MW00577159

TROUBLE IN PARADISE

Trouble Cat Mysteries #6

REBECCA BARRETT

KaliOka Press

Cover design by Cissy Hartley
Formatted by Priya Bhakta

For Larry McSween, the most special, special assistant.

The Naming of Cats is a difficult matter,
It isn't just one of your holiday games;
You may think at first I'm as mad as a hatter
When I tell you, a cat must have THREE
    DIFFERENT NAMES.

— T.S. ELIOT

CHAPTER ONE

"*Hello, Trout,*" *Ginger says.*

Instantly I rise from a light snooze on the window seat overlooking Petronia Street. I'm already salivating at the words from the proprietress of The Paradise Bed and Breakfast. But alas, the greeting is not for the vision of trout almandine already forming in my feline mind. It is, instead, addressed to a sandy-haired man in deck shoes, tattered khaki shorts, and a faded Hawaiian print shirt standing in the center of the foyer.

"*Ginger.*" *The man called Trout says.*

"*What brings you to the Paradise?*"

"*My morning charter. She was supposed to be at the marina at six.*"

"*One of mine?*" *Ginger asks as she slips from the high stool behind the reception desk.*

"*Yeah.*"

"*Name?*"

"*Liberty Anderson.*"

"*That would be the Toucan Suite. Not exactly your usual fare.*"

"*Why's that?*" *He asks.*

Ginger hesitates, then says, "Not the outdoor type, in my opinion."

Trout shrugs. "Her money spends like any other."

Trout exudes a mixture of scents; sea air, cotton dried in the sun, fish. I admit the latter is enough to draw me to examine his deck shoes.

"I see one of the Hemingway cats has strayed from home again." He places his hands on his hips and watches me as I investigate.

"He's not a museum cat." Ginger replies.

"Yours? You've gotten yourself a pet?"

"He belongs to my friend Tammy Lynn. She's on a cruise." Ginger leans her hip against the countertop. "They sailed yesterday."

Trout loses interest in me and crosses to the reception desk. He places an elbow on the high mahogany counter and runs his other hand through overlong, curling hair, and sighs. "You want to hustle up my charter?"

"Sure." Ginger picks up the phone receiver and punches in two numbers. She watches Trout as she listens to the clearly audible burring ring of the phone in the Toucan Suite. After several rings, she lets the receiver fall away from her ear and dangle from her curled fingers. She raises her eyebrows. "Did you try her cell phone?"

"For the past forty-five minutes. I decided the battery must be dead." He rubs the stubble on his chin. "You haven't seen her this morning, have you?"

Ginger hangs up the phone and shakes her head. "I've been up since five. She could have slipped out for a run while I was in the kitchen." She glances at the line of hooks on the wall behind the reception desk. "Her key's not here, so probably not." She hesitates, then says, "Coffee's on. You look like you could use a cup."

Ah, what's this? Do I detect a hint of interest on the part of Ginger? There is something in her voice that makes me wonder, a very subtle something, but there nevertheless. I turn my attention once again to Trout. What is it about this particular male biped that strikes a chord with the world-weary mistress of the Paradise Bed and Breakfast?

"*Do you think you could check to see if she's in her room?*" he asks.

Ginger straightens and leans ever so subtly away from him. "*I don't normally like to disturb my guests unless they request a wake-up call, but sure.*" *The something has disappeared from her voice. She takes the ring of master keys from a drawer.*

"*Thanks.*" *Trout jangles the change in his pocket.* "*I was counting on the booking. I'm a little pinched right now.*"

The faint lines on Ginger's forehead smooth, and she crosses the foyer to the stairs. I decide this is my opportunity to explore the Toucan Suite. The guest who booked it has been very standoffish and doesn't appear to have much affection for cats, me in particular. She has been very quick to close her door on my inquisitive nose. She even had the gall to tell me to "scat." Now I'm on a mission to gain access to her rooms just for the mischief of it. After all, she brought it upon herself.

Ginger knocks on the door of the Toucan Suite and waits, keys in hand. She glances down at me, arches an eyebrow and says, "Behave."

Moi? Whatever could she mean?

The knock goes unanswered, and Ginger frowns. She knocks harder. When there is still no answer, no sound of anyone stirring within the suite, she sighs.

I can see that she's hesitant to invade the premises of a guest at this early hour. It is odd that the occupant doesn't appear to hear the knocking at her door. That could be my own abilities coloring my impression of the situation. I can hear the crawling of a palmetto bug on the window sill of a room. One of the many talents that makes me such a superior sleuth.

Ginger glances down at me once more. The lack of any noise from the Toucan Suite seems to concern her. Either that or the desire to accommodate Trout overcomes her misgivings about her guest's privacy. She uses the master key and opens the door.

Sprawled across the counterpane of the bed is the guest I have labeled Birdbrain. I instantly catch a whiff of an unusual scent, one I haven't yet encountered in my young life. It's a pleasant smell. Underlying that rapidly fading aroma is one that is all too familiar to me in my young career as a detective. Liberty Anderson will never again shoo cats or any other creatures from her door. She is dead in Paradise.

Ginger hesitates on the threshold as if she too senses the absence of life in the pale body before her. She clears her throat. "Ms. Anderson."

I pad across the room to the foot of the bed where one of Liberty's hands trails to the floor. "Yeow." I sit and blink at Ginger.

"Liberty?" This time Ginger speaks louder and takes a couple of steps into the room. "Liberty Anderson!"

She moves quickly to the side of the woman in red sprawled across the bed and now sees the already clouding blue eyes open in an expression of what could be considered astonishment.

Ginger places two fingers against the artery in the woman's neck for a couple of heartbeats then backs away to the door. "Trout!" she calls down the stairs. "You'd better get up here."

GINGER'S HEART tapped a double beat when she looked down into the lifeless eyes of the woman in the Toucan Suite. She knew Liberty Anderson was dead even before she checked for a pulse.

This was only the third dead body Ginger had ever seen. The first had been her grandmother. Ginger had come home from school one day when she was nine and found her asleep on the front porch swing. At least, that's what she had thought at the time. The second death had been her mother. By the time Ginger arrived in Key West from Atlanta, Georgia, where she was attempting to make a career on the mainland, the impersonal process of the end of life had occurred. When Ginger saw her mother's body she looked nothing like the woman who had loved and nurtured her all her life. The only living thing from her past was the Paradise, and now, it had been tainted.

Ginger pushed a heavy wave of red curls back from her forehead and sighed. Liberty Anderson didn't look anything like her grandmother had or her mother. The sight of her open eyes made Ginger want to turn back the clock, to ignore Trout's request to rouse her guest from her slumber. But Liberty did not sleep.

Ginger's mind raced ahead with questions she knew the police would ask the moment they arrived. She needed to call them right away but she couldn't seem to move. Her gaze followed the movements of the black cat, Trouble, as he sniffed the dead woman's hand then leapt onto the bed and sniffed around her mouth.

Was this what had set the cat off in the middle of the night? Ginger thought back to the images of his meltdown at one in the morning. But Liberty hadn't been in her room then. The key to her suite had been on the board behind the registration desk.

She took a deep breath and released it slowly. Trout topped the stairs and came to stand beside her, looking into the room.

"Passed out?" he asked.

"Dead," she replied.

TROUT LOOKED from the dead woman to Ginger then back again. He didn't need to enter the room to know that Ginger was right in her assessment of the situation. There is a stillness in death that's like no other; and, with the exception of the black cat, there was no life emanating from the room.

He leaned his body weight away from the doorway, an involuntary movement brought on by other deaths and other lonely hotel rooms. Except for the red dress, this could have been Missy. The image before him mirrored that horrible scene in that flea-bag of a motel in Tallahassee four years ago.

The police would need to be called, and the process of a suspicious death would begin. He didn't plan to stick around for the formalities.

He jangled the change in his pocket. "Was she ill, do you know? A heart condition or something?"

"I've no idea. She's just a tourist doing the tourist thing."

"The tourist thing?"

"Sleeping late, out half the night, dressed for..." Ginger hesitated. The woman was dead, for Pete's sake.

"Action?" Trout suggested.

"She was having a good time. Let's just leave it at that."

"Did she bring anyone back to the Paradise?"

"No."

"You sure?"

Ginger hesitated. "Pretty sure. I think I would have heard them."

"All right, then. I guess we should call 911." He watched as the black cat worked his way down the length of Liberty's body, sniffing the whole way. "And get that damn cat away from her."

The cat paused at the woman's left foot and fixated on her big toe, then lost interest.

Unwilling to break the plane of the door casing, to be drawn into the drama of unexpected death and loss, Trout made a hissing sound through his teeth in an effort to scare the cat off the bed. The cat flattened his ears and sniffed one last time. He then sat back on his haunches and observed Trout through the narrow slits of his emerald green eyes.

Ginger gave a small shake of her head. "Trouble," she said, "off the bed."

The cat called Trouble turned his gaze to Ginger, blinked three times, and hopped down from the bed. He made his way silently to Liberty's purse and its spilled contents on the floor by the dressing table. After he examined all the items, he padded off into the bathroom.

"Crazy cat," Trout said. Neither he nor Ginger made a move to set in motion what they both knew had to happen. It occurred to Trout that a dead body at the bed and breakfast couldn't be good for Ginger's business. Late summer wasn't the most lucrative time of the year for either of them. Fewer tourists were willing to risk a ruined vacation in Key West at the height of hurricane season. Parents were getting children ready to return to school, and retirees didn't want to be in the sub-tropics when temperatures ranged in the high nineties, and the humidity was off the charts.

It was as if the inability to rally to action lifted from each of them at the same time. Trout and Ginger turned toward the head of the stairs.

When they reached the ground floor, Trout looked at Ginger. "You okay?"

She nodded.

He noted the paleness around her lips. He had hoped to skip out while she phoned the police. He didn't want to get tangled up with an investigation. After all, he didn't know the dead woman. Not really. She was simply a charter to him.

When Ginger reached for the phone on the reception desk, he noted the slight tremble of her hand. He had left it too late. His window of opportunity to escape the mayhem of all a suspicious death entailed had slammed shut. He couldn't leave her alone to deal with a dead body now that he knew how shaken she was.

He had known Ginger since he first landed in Key West almost two years ago from upstate. After a six-month hiatus he thought of as his lost period, he had looked around for a means to support himself. He crewed on a couple of deep sea fishing boats for the remainder of that year and decided this was the life for him.

During that first year, he had seen Ginger around town, more often than not at the Smokin' Tuna, a restaurant and bar frequented in the after-hours, off-season, by locals. She, and a couple of other small establishment owners, had been willing to keep fliers of his charter company available for interested guests.

On several occasions in the past, when he was nearing the end of a six-pack, Trout acknowledged to himself that he was more than a little attracted to her. In his more sober moments, he never allowed his thoughts to linger in such treacherous waters. Trout had purposely chosen the life of a loner, and Key West was an ideal setting for like-minded people.

The black cat caught Trout's eye as he came down the stairs. He paused on the third step from the bottom and sat, curling his tail around his front paws.

Trout listened to Ginger's end of the phone conversation with the police. They had her stay on the line, so he went through to the kitchen and poured each of them a cup of coffee. He hesitated over the blueberry muffins but decided it would be unseemly to take one under the circumstances.

GINGER ACCEPTED the steaming cup of coffee from Trout with a nod of thanks. She had hung up on the 911 operator after assuring her that she wasn't in any danger and that she wasn't going anywhere.

As she sipped the hot brew, she realized her hands were no longer shaking and her mind was reviewing the details of the room when she first opened the door to the Toucan Suite. The image that stuck in her mind was the lone red shoe that rested on its side on the floor just below where Liberty Anderson's left foot rested half on and half off the bed.

"Is this your first dead body?" Trout asked.

Ginger cleared her throat but in the end only shook her head.

The sound of a police siren grew louder as it approached from the direction of Truman Avenue. She took another sip of coffee and placed the cup on the registration counter.

"Did you smell anything in the room?" she asked Trout.

He thought for a second, his forehead creased with a frown, and shook his head. "No." He looked down at Ginger. "Like perfume you mean?"

"Not that exactly." She glanced toward the front door where two uniform police officers were entering the building. "It was an unusual scent, very faint." Her shoulders lifted in a slight shrug. "Probably just my imagination."

Ginger knew Trout didn't want to be there, that the thought of becoming entangled in the investigation had him half-way to the door. His desire to be gone was evident in the tension in his body, the restless darting of his gaze around the foyer of the Paradise. She was grateful that he had remained with her, had given her time to recover from the initial shock of her discovery. "Sorry about all this," she said.

Trout jangled his change once again. "What are friends for, right?"

Friends. They were friends. She had felt drawn to him the

first time she saw him balancing precariously on a bar stool at the Bull and Whistle, his head in his hand. His hollowed-out eyes and morning-after shakes from hard drinking had, with time, given way to a permanent tan that made his pale blue eyes startling when you first saw him. His frame had filled out with hard work and the slow return of his appetite.

Whatever had driven him to abandon his former life and bury himself in the Florida Keys was still a mystery to her. It was a common state of being for many who drifted down the state seeking some intangible something, or seeking nothing at all.

Ginger didn't know which it was with Trout.

The two policemen crossed the foyer, and Ginger gave them a brief summary of the situation. One of them went up the stairs to stand guard over the body in the Toucan Suite while the other separated her and Trout. She saw Trout's wistful glance at the front entrance of the Paradise as the policeman motioned for him to wait in the kitchen. A twinge of guilt tugged at her. She should have sent him on his way the moment she got off the phone with the police. Now it was too late.

About ten minutes later, Duncan Moore strolled through the beveled glass front doors of the Paradise. One of the uniformed policemen intercepted him, obviously giving him the run-down on the situation.

Of all the people they could have sent, Ginger thought. She had mentally prepared herself for Ricki Lofton, a detective with the police force and a friend. Instead she had Duncan.

"Ginger." Duncan shrugged his shoulders in that forward roll of his. "Got a bit of a complication, I hear."

Duncan and Ginger had fallen into a short-lived relation-ship a couple of years back when she first returned to Key

West from the greater world of the mainland to take over the Paradise. He was a handsome man with his dark hair beginning to gray at the temples, deep blue eyes, and a compact but solid physique. The problem with Duncan was he had a habit of falling into short-lived relationships.

Ginger had long since gotten over Duncan. In truth, she had known going in the kind of man he was. Their relationship had been more about lust than love. She had known that going in, too. At the time, they had met a need for each other. His presence on the case as the detective wasn't ideal.

"Duncan. How've you been?"

"Same old, same old."

The humor in the situation struck Ginger and she laughed. "I don't doubt that one bit, Duncan. Not one bit."

He grinned. "You know me, Ginger. I get restless."

"Who's on the line now?"

He shrugged again. "Free floating at the moment."

"When aren't you free floating?"

"You're looking good."

"If forty looks good on anyone."

"You know what they say. Forty is the new thirty."

"I'm a long way from thirty."

"Yeah, but you're not forty either. More like thirty-five, right?"

"Close enough."

"Whatever. You still look good. Things seem to be going well for you."

"If you don't consider the dead body in my most expensive suite."

"Yeah. About that, who is she?"

"Liberty Anderson. She checked in four days ago."

"You found her in her room dead?"

"Yes."

"Door locked?"

"Yes."

"Help me out here, Ginger." A note of exasperation underlined his words.

Ginger crossed her arms at waist level. "I don't know when she came in last night. She wasn't in her room at one."

"And how do you know that?"

"The cat started yowling."

"Cat? You got a cat?"

"No. He belongs to a friend."

As if on cue, Trouble sauntered into the reception area from the direction of the kitchen. He gave Duncan an assessing look and continued on to the stairs.

"A friend, huh?"

"Do you want to hear the rest of the story?"

"Sure, sure."

"Ms. Anderson didn't like cats."

"Imagine that."

"So, I came to see what had set him off. I didn't want him disturbing the guests."

"What set him off?"

"I don't know. He wanted to get into Ms. Anderson's room. He kept pacing outside the door; then he would stop and reach his paw up to the door knob and bat at it."

"You let him in?"

"Of course not. I picked him up and took him to my room."

"So how did you know she wasn't in for the night?"

"The key. I have a card reader for the front entrance, but I've never changed out the locks on the rooms. I use the big old-fashioned keys so people don't walk off with them."

"I remember."

Ginger frowned. "Anyway, her key was still on the hook."

"Was it there when you first turned in?"

Ginger stared at the row of hooks and keys on a board behind the reception desk trying to evoke the image of it as it was when she made her rounds before bedtime. She couldn't be sure. "I don't know."

Duncan watched the cat sitting on the third step of the stairs. "What made you check her room this morning?"

When she didn't respond immediately, Duncan forgot about the cat and looked at Ginger. She glanced away from his scrutiny and down at the floor.

"Trout," she said.

"Trout?"

Ginger squared her shoulders and looked into Duncan's eyes. She could almost see him searching through all the facts and detritus that is the mind of a cop. "He bought Big Mouth's rig last year."

Duncan nodded absently, his mental process finally settling on a memory. "The guy in the kitchen." He thought for a moment. "What did he have to do with it?"

"She was his charter for this morning. When she didn't show up, he came looking for her."

"Why would he do that? Why not just charge her for the missed charter?"

"He's not like that?"

"Like what? A good businessman?"

"He wouldn't just take her money."

Duncan watched her, a look of speculation in his eyes. "So, he came looking for her."

Ginger nodded. "I called the room and got no answer." She hesitated. "Then I decided to check her room."

"You said the door was locked."

"Yes. I used my pass key." Ginger looked away from Duncan's probing regard. "There she was, lying across the bed, fully clothed. Except for the shoe."

"The shoe?"

"The left shoe had fallen off her foot. It was on the floor."

"How did you know she was dead?"

"I didn't at first, but when she didn't respond when I called her name," Ginger gave her head a small shake, "it was just so still. Too still. I just knew."

"Did you enter the room?"

She nodded. "I checked her pulse at her throat, but I already knew. The eyes..." she looked away again.

"Yeah." Duncan was silent for a moment. "Did you touch anything?"

"No."

"How about the boat captain?"

"He never entered the room."

"Okay." He touched her lightly on the upper arm, not quite a pat but only long enough to offer reassurance. "She might have been diabetic or had a heart condition or something. Let's not read anything into it."

"But she's so young. She looks to be in her late twenties."

"Yeah, well, don't worry, okay? Old age isn't the only cause of death. The coroner will figure it out."

Ginger nodded.

"Who else was working last night?"

"No one. Jules works every other night for me manning the desk and phone. If a guest needs something, whoever has the shift takes care of it. There's a daybed in the little office behind the desk." She indicated the door behind her with a jerk of her head. "Last night was my night on duty. I sleep in my room but have a monitor so I can hear what's going on in the foyer."

"Like a baby monitor?"

She nodded.

"And you didn't hear her come in last night?"

"No."

"Any other staff on the premises?"

Ginger shook her head. "The bar closes at eleven, so Harry left about eleven-fifteen, eleven-twenty. Angela doesn't come in until seven each morning. I start the coffee and do the set up for breakfast. She comes in to start serving. Afterwards she helps with the cleaning until noon. When she got here this morning, the first policemen on the scene had just arrived. They sent her home."

"That's your whole staff?"

"Yes. Four people. I only serve breakfast and finger sand-wiches at tea. There's the tiki bar out by the pool, of course, but I only have Harry out there when it's more likely to be busy. Otherwise I monitor it while seeing to other needs of my guests. If anyone gets hungry at night, there's a food station in the butler's pantry. They can get a soft drink, water, cookies. Things like that."

"That's a lean operation."

"What can I say? It's what I can afford. Besides, with the two cottages that's only seven rooms."

"How many guests are registered right now?"

"Four rooms. A total of six guests. Well, except for Liberty, that makes five, I guess."

"I'll want their names. Save me the trouble later if there's anything to be concerned about."

Ginger hesitated, uncertain as to whether or not she should simply hand over such information but rationalized it wasn't just anyone she was giving it to. "Sure," she said and went behind the reception desk and booted up the computer. With a few key strokes, she printed out a list for Duncan.

He scanned down the list, folded it, and put it in his inside coat pocket as he turned toward the kitchen.

"Don't you want to see the body?"

He glanced back at Ginger. "In due course."

TROUT WASHED down the last of the blueberry muffin with the dregs in his coffee cup as the kitchen door swung open.

He recognized the man who sauntered into the room and gave him the once over. He had seen him here and there around Key West, mainly at the Smokin' Tuna. At the time, Trout had figured him for a cop. There was something about the body language that was universal.

"Trout," the man said. "Is that some kind of nickname?"

Trout nodded. "Armentrout. Richardson."

The cop whistled softly. "That's some moniker. Your folks must have really loved you."

Trout made no reply. He didn't plan on being drawn into a play at being best buds in a relationship he knew could only end as adversarial.

The cop let the silence draw out. He went to the coffee maker and poured himself a cup. After a tentative sip he said, "You found the body?"

"No." Trout waited until the detective looked up at him. "Ginger found her."

"I hear you're a very conscientious kind of guy."

"How's that?"

"You always go in search of fares that don't show up?"

"Not always."

"Just this time."

Trout said nothing.

"How well did you know Ms. Anderson?"

"Not at all. Not really." Trout jangled the change in his pocket.

"Which is it? Not at all or not really?"

Trout sighed and shook his head. "I saw her last night, but I didn't know she was my charter until this morning. When we found her."

The detective did a shoulder roll then caught a thumb in the waistband of his slacks. "By *saw her*, you mean what? Exactly."

"She was at the Bull and Whistle. At the bar making friends with anyone and everyone."

"And you noticed her particularly because?"

"The red dress. The whole Marilyn Monroe look she had going on."

"But you didn't know who she was."

"She said her name was Alice."

The detective watched Trout a moment longer then took another sip of his coffee. "So, you didn't just see her, you spoke to her. What else did you do if I might be so bold as to ask."

"Nothing."

"You didn't buy her drinks? Take a spin on the dance floor? Show her the sights of Key West?"

Trout tamped down his rising anger at the detective's tone. This was exactly what he knew would happen if he got sucked into this investigation. Once again, his motives would be called into question, his life placed under a microscope. "Look. I was sitting at the bar, she came in and sat next to me and we chatted. She wanted to know where the Oriole was. Said her taxi driver told her about it and she was all fired up to experience the real night life of Key West."

"And the two of you trundled along to the Oriole."

"No. I finished my drink and headed back to the boat. I had an early charter."

"And you didn't know it was with the woman at the bar?"

"Like I said."

"Why would she say her name was Alice?"

"Can't help you there. Maybe she was doing the Vegas thing."

"What Vegas thing?"

"You know. What happens in Vegas stays in Vegas."

"Huh." The detective drained his cup of coffee and eyed the blueberry muffins. "Strange coincidence, wouldn't you say?"

"What's that?"

"That you should run into a woman you didn't know, with whom you had an early morning charter, on the very night before she's found dead in her room."

"Key West is a small place."

"Not that small."

CHAPTER TWO

I must confess a certain vanity when it comes to bipeds. Generally, they find me charming and actually seek out my company. Detective Moore, however, is unmoved by my sleek black coat and winsome ways. I doubt even my British accent could sway him...if he could hear it.

One of his policemen has corralled me and dumped me unceremoniously into Ginger's arms with the admonition to keep me from under foot. He doesn't appreciate the fact that I am his best bet to solve this case. A youth spent watching Benedict Cumberbatch as Sherlock has reinforced my natural ability inherited from my dear old Da, the famous black cat detective, Familiar.

Moore's attitude toward me is of small consequence. It is the less than thorough approach to the circumstances of this case that causes me anxiety. To the police, Liberty Anderson's death is a mystery but not yet a crime. I can only hope the coroner is more astute and more thorough.

I regret my fit of pique last night outside Liberty's door. It was a childish prank, I confess, to gain access to her room. Let's call it boredom and be done with it. Had I but known she was in danger. But, how could I? There was no hint of it at the time, no telltale scent lingering *in the air. Nothing in her behavior prior to the fact to indicate anything other than that she was a bird out to have a good time.*

Trout has been sent on his way by the police with a relieved expression on his face. I find I can tolerate his company. He understood my request for nourishment and gave me one of Ginger's blueberry muffins while he waited to be interviewed by Moore. A dollop of jam would have been appreciated but it's early days yet. I should be able to whip him into shape quickly. After all, Tammy and Aiden will be away for seven more days.

For once Tammy is doing something simply for the pleasure of it, a little vacation from her duties as owner and procurer for the Book Basket in Wetumpka. She thought this would be a nice vacation for me here in the Conch Republic of Key West, but as usual I find myself where I am needed with a mystery to solve.

A piece of yellow tape has been placed across the casing of the closed door of the Toucan Suite. Ginger is distracted, and perhaps a bit distressed, by the demands of two of her guests to be checked out of their rooms immediately. The fact that they will have to remain in Key West until the police determine the cause of death has them in a hostile mood. Not even the fact that their reservations would have kept them in town for three more nights seems to bear weight with them.

It appears it will be up to me to solve this case and restore Ginger's business. For a moment, I had hopes that Trout would jump into the fray. He's an interesting one, a bit of a mystery himself. I'm sure I'll soon discover the root of his dismay at these unsettling events. Does he simply have an aversion to death? Or is he hiding out from some legal entanglement from his past? Time will tell.

There is chemistry between him and Ginger. Perhaps he'll come around. In the meantime, I'll check out the area, learn the lay of the land, see how someone could have gained access to the locked Toucan Suite for I have no doubt that the murderer laid in wait for his victim. Access, that's the tricky question, but I shall find the answer.

I slip through the front door of the Paradise on the heels of a police-man. The grounds of the bed and breakfast are lush with foliage and I'm briefly distracted by a rather large iguana. He must be at least two feet long, tail to nose. We engage in a Mexican standoff, his beady eyes unflinching, but one flick of my tail and he darts away.

At the rear of the house is a narrow back porch that runs the length of the building. On the southeast corner a staircase runs up the east side to the second floor. At the top of these stairs, lying on his back, sprawled across the landing, is a very fat, gray cat. Beside him is a petite gray with white markings.

As I top the stairs, the petite gray ceases her complaining and turns her crossed-eyed gaze on me. Obviously curious about the cause of the sudden silence, the fat cat opens his eyes.

"Who're you?" he asks.

"Trouble."

He wriggles and squirms until he can get his feet under him and he strolls over to me. "We won't have any trouble around here, you hear?"

I suppress a sigh. "My name is Trouble."

The female begins to purr, moves beside the fat cat, and touches her nose to mine. Her eyes are very disconcerting.

"I'm Megs," she says.

The fat cat muscles her to the side. "Where'd you come from?"

"Wetumpka."

"What's that? Wetumpka?"

"A city."

"Oh."

They stare at me as if I had said the moon.

I know Ginger doesn't own any pets. "Where'd you come from?"

The female motions with her head toward the east. "The museum. We're Hemingway cats."

The tone of her voice suggests I should be impressed by this revela-tion. When she gets no reaction from me she holds up her paw, a boda-

cious seven toes displayed for my edification, and glances at the fat cat. "Show him, Bartholomew," she says.

Bartholomew grunts and lies back down, ignoring me and Megs.

She sidles up to me and rubs along the length of my body, purring all the while. "So, what brings you to Key West?"

I confess vanity made me say it. "Murder."

Bartholomew lifts his large head, opens his eyes, and stares at me. Megs does a funny little quick step, right paw over left paw, left paw over right, three times in rapid succession.

Still unimpressed, Bartholomew says, "Who'd you kill, a mouse?" Then he grins.

That rather deflates my ego. "No one," I say, "I'm a detective."

"Wow." Megs moves right up in my face. "You mean you solve crimes? Catch murderers?"

"Precisely. You may have heard of my father, Familiar?"

Bartholomew grunts, lies his head down, closes his eyes, and rolls onto his back.

"Are you on a case? Are you on a case?" Megs does her little dance.

Normally I play my cards close to my vest, but given that Megs and Bartholomew appear to use the premises as they wish, I see the benefit of putting them in the know.

"Where were you both last night?"

"You are on a case!" Meg's crossed-eyes almost twirl like a whirly-gig in her excitement. "Is it murder?"

"Yes, I'm on a case and it's most definitely murder."

"Oh, oh, oh! Can I help? Can I be your sidekick?"

"What you can do is tell me if you were on the grounds of the Paradise last night and anything you saw."

"Yes!" Megs does her little dance. "We were a..."

"Megs!" Bartholomew growls and rocks back and forth until his great weight shifts and he is once again on his feet. "We were at the museum, in our beds in the cat house. We weren't spying on anyone."

"Oh, right." Megs says, as she looks from me to Bartholomew then back to me. *"We weren't violating the court order. Honest."*

"Court order? What court order?" Hello. What have I uncovered?

"What are you talking about?" Bartholomew asks. *"We're cats. We know nothing of legal wranglings and officious secret agents."* He suddenly discovers a need to groom between his toes.

Megs lowers her gaze and moves to the corner of the landing, gazing out across the back lawn. She won't look at me.

Well, something is afoot here, but it must take a back seat to the matter at hand. Whatever these two know could be vital to finding a killer.

GINGER BALANCED the stack of clean linens on her hip as she fished in her pocket for the key to the newly-vacated Flamenco Suite. It was the middle room of three on the front of the Paradise, and one of the most expensive because of the gallery access. The loss of three nights' occupancy would hurt. She could only hope the Williamsons would decide not to do a review on any of the travel websites.

Just as she inserted the key in the lock, she heard the muffled tones of a ringing cell phone. It was coming from the Toucan Suite next door.

She placed the linens on a hallway table and held her ear to the door listening. The phone continued to ring insistently. She stepped back and eyed the crime scene tape along the door casing.

"Crap." With the key, she sliced through the tape and entered the room. As soon as she stepped over the threshold the phone stopped ringing but not before Ginger had an idea of where the sound came from.

She had already violated Duncan's instructions that no one

enter the room so she might as well go all in and find the phone. The dying ring had echoed from the area of the dressing table.

The police had taken all of Liberty's beauty aids. All that remained was a box of tissues and a handheld mirror. Ginger started to open the drawers on either side of the knee hole of the dressing table but stopped herself just in time. Fingerprints, she thought. Then she decided that was a ludicrous idea. Her guest had died because of some health issue. The thought that it could be anything else was ridiculous. Still, she left the drawers alone and got down on her knees. The most logical place to find a cell phone would be in a woman's purse and since Liberty's purse had fallen to the floor and spilled...

Ah, there it was, all the way in the back recess under the dressing table. Someone on the police force would catch the devil for this oversight.

Ginger reached into the dark corner and could just touch the phone. Finally, she got a clothes hanger from the armoire and fished it out. She stood and stared at the face of it. She debated with herself the wisdom of checking out the call log. Maybe it was a family member trying to reach Liberty. Ginger's thumb hovered over the large button briefly before she gave in to the impulse. The phone's screen sprang to life at her touch. Not password protected, then, she realized.

She went to the log and looked at the incoming calls. A number labeled Boss showed seven calls. Ginger clicked on the messages and listened to an increasingly angry male voice demanding that Liberty check in with the office. In the last message he said, "The federal government isn't paying you to be on vacation. And don't try to deny it. I've seen the photos plastered all over Facebook. Call me if you still want to have a job when you get back to DC!"

This was an interesting turn of events, Ginger thought. She flipped through the icons and opened Facebook. There, bigger than life, was Liberty Anderson, smiling for the camera. Ginger scrolled through several posts. She understood what had Liberty's boss so angry if she was, in fact, in Key West on business. Without question, a lot of partying had occurred since she arrived in the Conch Republic.

She switched from Facebook to the camera on the phone. At the twelfth picture in, she stopped. There staring at her was a photograph of Trout. He was at a bar somewhere. She couldn't tell where. He was smiling at the camera.

Ginger sat on the side of the bed and let the hand holding the phone rest in her lap as she stared into space. Trout hadn't told her that he knew Liberty. Which, in her opinion, would have been a given since the two of them found her dead on the morning he was supposed to take her out in his boat.

Her mind raced through what she knew of Liberty. Ginger had assumed she was in Key West on vacation. All her actions indicated that to be the case. And, yes, people in town for work usually took the time to see the sights and enjoy themselves, but Ginger hadn't thought that was the case with Liberty. She had slept in, dressed in shorts and halter tops or playful sundresses. So, what was this job?

Ginger went back to the phone for any clues. Most of the phone numbers had the same area code as the one for her boss. She quickly Googled the three digits and discovered it was for the Washington, DC area. It was safe to assume then that Liberty lived and worked in or near the capitol. A few numbers in the call log were local, probably restaurants or tourist attractions. Liberty's Facebook page was a testament to the fact that she had hit just about every spot from Mallory Pier to the Southernmost Point marker. Few tourists had the stamina for that much partying except kids. Liberty was young but she wasn't a kid.

The photos on the camera were some of the same ones posted on Facebook but there were tons of others. A lot of them were of the Hemingway House Museum and the Hemingway cats. In fact, there were dozens of photos of cats all over Key West.

It was the shots of Westward Harbor Marina at the beginning of the string of pictures of Key West that stilled Ginger's scrolling finger. Trout docked at the Westward Harbor Marina and while there was no photo of his boat, it was odd that Liberty would photograph that particular marina and so early in her stay. Had she gone looking for a boat to charter? Had Trout met her four days ago? She thought back over their conversation of the morning. It was true that he never specifically said he didn't know his fare but it was implied. She had to find out why he had lied to her.

Ginger stood and ran a hand along the bed to smooth where she had been sitting. She slipped the iPhone into her back pocket, glanced around the room, and left. As she was locking the Toucan Suite, a door toward the back end of the landing opened and her guest in the Bird Cage, Annette Benoit, stepped into the hallway.

"*Bonjour*," Annette said as she passed Ginger. At the top of the stairs she turned back and asked. "Any calls for me?"

"No." Ginger picked up the stack of clean linens. "Still no calls."

The woman nodded and went down the stairs.

Ginger's heart thumped in her chest like a machine gun. She would never make a secret agent, she decided. The thought of getting caught in the act of trespassing in a room blocked off with crime scene tape, a room she had been told specifically to leave under lock and key, had scared the pants off her. Would Annette think anything of her coming out of the Toucan Suite? Probably not. Annette was too caught up in her own situation, whatever that was, to pay attention. In fact, the blond seemed oblivious to everything around her and had barely batted an eye when the Paradise was overrun with police in the aftermath of the discovery of Liberty's body.

Still, Ginger waited until she heard the front door of the Paradise close behind her guest. She returned the linens to the hallway table and hurried down the stairs. At the back of the bed and breakfast she had her personal quarters with a small office nook. She settled into her desk chair and scrolled down the numbers in Liberty's phone.

Her laptop was slow to boot up but finally the Google search page sprang onto the screen. She sat back in the chair. What was she doing? She should immediately call Duncan and tell him about the phone. It should be in the hands of the police. There was probably a simple explanation of why Liberty had a photo of Trout. The truth was, Ginger couldn't think of one. Because she couldn't think of a reason for a dead woman to have a photo of Trout and the marina where he docked his boat, she had to find out what Liberty had been doing in Key West. She didn't stop to question why it was so important to her to know.

On her laptop Ginger keyed in a search for the first of the local numbers in the phone's log. She needed to know where Liberty had been and what she'd been doing. Trouble hopped onto the desk and watched the computer screen.

"Where'd you come from?" Ginger asked as she scratched between his ears. "I haven't seen you in hours."

Trouble stretched his head in the direction of her magic fingers but he never took his eyes off the computer screen.

. . .

TROUT BLEW a fine layer of sawdust from the mahogany plank
and ran his hand along the smooth wood. To pay his dockage
fees he helped Sawyer around the marina with manual labor.
Sawyer's current passion was a vintage 1930s era J class sailboat
built by the Defoe Boat Works. Trout had been sanding the
deck for two weeks.

He straightened from his task and as he wiped his cramped
fingers with a rag, he let his gaze travel over the long line of
docked boats. Walking down the pier toward him was Ginger,
the afternoon sun creating a fiery halo of her dark red curls,
the floral print wrap skirt she wore exposing a bit of long, tan
leg with each stride. Behind her trotted the black cat.

Trout sighed, dusted the fine powder from the front of his
shirt and shorts. This was not a good thing. He swung down
the ladder to the pier and watched her approach. When she
was still ten feet from him, she stopped.

"Why didn't you tell me?" she asked.

"Tell you what?"

"That you knew Liberty."

"Because it had nothing to do with the situation."

"So, you thought it would be better for me to be blind-
sided?" Her stance was defiant, a real squared off, no nonsense
posture.

"Look," Trout said, "I don't know what the detective told
you but..."

"Duncan didn't tell me anything."

Trout hesitated. "Then how...?" He angled his head a little
to the right in a puzzled look.

"It doesn't matter how I know. You should have told me."

"Why?"

"Because..." she shook her head, raised and dropped her hands in a helpless gesture. "Because she's dead."

Trout glanced toward the shore and the marina office, then returned his gaze to Ginger. "Come on," he motioned with his hand back down the pier from the direction she had come. "Let's find a little privacy, okay?"

Ginger stepped to the side so he could pass by her and they walked about fifteen yards to where his boat, the *Baby Buddha*, was berthed. After a slight hesitation, Ginger climbed aboard. Trout nodded toward a canvas deck chair then went below. He came back on deck with two cold bottles of beer. He handed one to her and sat in a second chair.

"Now," he said, "tell me what you think you know."

Ginger shook her head. "It doesn't work that way, Trout. You need to tell me how you know Liberty Anderson. Tell me why a party girl chartered a fishing expedition. Why you?"

Trout nodded. "Good enough." He settled into his chair, his feet up on the transom, and faced the westernly sun. "Sawyer got a call from a woman wanting the use of a deep-water boat for a morning trip into the Gulf. She wasn't interested in fishing, just needed the transport and privacy. She wanted a sunrise kind of experience she told him. He gave her my number. He knew I could use the money." Trout took a long pull on his beer, wiped the back of his hand across his mouth, and continued. "She told me she would pay the regular fee for a half-day fishing excursion."

"If she wasn't interested in fishing, what was the purpose?"

Trout shook his head but continued to gaze into the distance. "Can't say. Maybe she just liked being out on the ocean. Maybe she wanted to commune with nature. I didn't ask."

"Why didn't you tell me you knew her?"

"Because I didn't. At least, I didn't know I knew her until I saw her sprawled across the bed." He took another drink then started peeling the label on the beer bottle. "The only contact I had with her was a phone call. At least, that's what I thought until I looked into the room. I'd been sitting at the bar at the Bull and Whistle when she came in last night. She was in high spirits, friendly to a fault, taking pictures with her phone with everyone in the place. When she sat next to me, she asked me to smile and she snapped my picture. Said her name was Alice."

When Trout said nothing more, Ginger prodded him. "And?"

"And nothing. Other people came in, she got involved with them for a bit, bought drinks, took lots of pictures, and then she left."

Ginger's forehead creased into frown lines. "So, she just said, hi, my name is Alice. That's it?"

"Pretty much," Trout said.

"What happens in Vegas."

Trout cut his eyes in her direction. "My thoughts exactly."

"Still, that's a strange coincidence."

"The cops think so, too."

"I don't know why you didn't tell me this morning."

Trout was silent. Finally, he heaved a heavy sigh, took another drink, and said. "I know how these things go. I didn't want to be in that position again. I thought that the autopsy would show she had some kind of condition, or maybe alcohol poisoning. She was drinking heavily and already tipsy when she got to the Bull and Whistle. I figured if I just kept my mouth shut, things would sort themselves."

"You said *again*. What does that mean?"

He pulled a long strip of the label from the bottle and let it drift to the deck of the boat. "Another girl, another death, another lifetime. It didn't matter that I didn't have anything to do with what happened to her, either. The police thought it was too much of a coincidence that I was her therapist and that I found her body."

"I'm sorry."

Trout emptied the bottle with one last chug, set it on the deck, and leaned further back in the chair, his eyes closed. "Yeah, well, that's life."

Trouble yowled softly. Trout opened one eye and saw him sitting on the transom inches from his propped feet. "So much for the luck of a black cat," he said. "Then again, it's Friday."

I AM NOT SUPERSTITIOUS. The old sailors' tales of luck of a ship's black cat are just that. The utility of such seafaring felines in the control of vermin is the well from which such beliefs spring. If it gives comfort to those who venture onto the high seas then who am I to judge, but, really, the idea of Friday being an unlucky day to set sail is no more valid than all the other taboos of me and my black brethren. Humans. What can I say. They'll believe almost anything.

The feline ability to judge character, however, is spot on. I daresay Ginger has many questions concerning Trout's reference to other girls and other deaths. It would be preferable to know the facts but on the face of things, I can't at the moment think Trout is our killer. Still, it doesn't hurt to investigate every possibility. I could be wrong in my assessment of him. More likely, I'm wrong in thinking I could be wrong for I am pretty much infallible. This is not vanity but merely fact.

I think I'll take a stroll around the Baby Buddha *while Ginger and Trout await the sunset. They seem comfortable in the silence that has fallen over them since his revelation. I sense questions on Ginger's part but she's content for the moment to wait. Patience, a good skill for a detective to have. I confess I find her initiative and her instincts so far to be superior to that of the local authorities.*

The Baby Buddha *is a rather nice boat. It isn't as large as a convertible but still it has a flying bridge and a cuddy cabin that's more spacious than some. Two bipeds could sleep quite comfortably here for a night or two as long as the water wasn't too rough. They don't have the natural agility and inner balance that felines rely on to keep motion from being a problem.*

There's nothing of interest below deck except a padlocked cabinet in the galley beneath the banquet seat. Probably where Trout stores valuables when his boat is unattended. I can't say I have much faith in the lock to the cabin proper. With all this valuable fishing gear on board I would expect something more substantial. Then, again, I guess since Trout makes this his home, there isn't too much to worry about. He seems adequate to deal with anyone cruising the docks for an easy score. That, and the fact that access to the pier requires a code, should deter all but the most desperate.

From the flying bridge of the Baby Buddha *there's a nice view of the marina. I think I could become accustomed to life on the sea. Perhaps it's only the temptation of the contents of the live bait well that has me thinking such thoughts. I hope there's fish for dinner.*

GINGER AND TROUT finished their beers and she refrained from questioning him about his past or anything she had learned from Liberty's phone. She struggled with whether or not to tell him about finding it or turning it in to Duncan. As the sun set below the horizon she still hadn't made up her mind.

She was reluctant to disturb the harmony they had found. The truth was that she liked his nearness, liked the gentle bounce of the boat. When Trout refused her invitation to walk back to the Paradise for dinner, he declined without any excuses as to why. Good enough, she thought. It had been a rough day for both of them.

Trouble padded along beside her as she wound her way through the streets of Key West, taking the shortest route back to her bed and breakfast. She hadn't noticed him following her when she left the Paradise earlier in the day. Her mind had been so caught up with the happenings of the morning that it hadn't occurred to her to be more aware of him and his needs.

Now, as they made their way home she decided he was a smart cat, smart enough to follow her lead. He was probably hungry, too. Unaccustomed to caring for a pet as she was didn't excuse her neglect. She'd have to see what she could whip up for him. Tammy had warned her he was a finicky eater.

A man with thick curly brown hair, a slender build, and horn-rimmed glasses met her on the sidewalk in front of the Paradise. He came from the south as she came from the north. They both turned into the walkway leading up to the front porch. Trouble immediately began to twine around the man's legs, nearly tripping him in the process.

"Sorry," Ginger said as she paused at the bottom of the steps and smiled. "He's usually not such a pain. Can I help you?" she asked.

The man stopped as well, barely missing Trouble's tail. "Are you staying here?" he asked.

"I'm the owner," she replied.

"Oh. Well, then maybe you can. I'm looking for a Ms. Anderson."

Ginger was silent for a heartbeat. "Liberty Anderson?"

He nodded. "Yes. I understand she's staying here."

Ginger wasn't sure how to proceed. Should she tell him

that Liberty was dead? Was that something Duncan would want her to keep under wraps until he knew the cause of death? She decided on a half-truth. "She isn't here at the moment and I don't think she'll be available tonight. Could I say who called by? Or maybe I could take a message?"

The man hesitated then shook his head. "Never mind," he said. "I'll catch up with her another time."

Frantically Ginger searched for a gambit that would garner more information. "Did you know her well?"

He shook his head. "We only recently met." Then he turned and retraced his steps away from the Paradise.

Ginger watched his departure and she watched as Trouble followed him all the way to where the walkway of the Paradise met the sidewalk. As the man disappeared into the twilight, she tried to think what to do but couldn't think of anything.

Jules looked up from the book he was reading at the reception desk when she and Trouble came through the front door. "Hi," he said. "There's a couple of messages for you from Detective Moore." He held out two pink slips of paper.

"Thanks. Everything else quiet?"

"Everything except the Bird Cage. She's called down twice asking if she's had any messages." He rolled his eyes. "As if I wouldn't put the call through."

"Doesn't she have a cell phone? I distinctly remember seeing her use one a couple of days ago."

"I think so." Jules scratched his beard. He had little facial hair and was trying desperately for a beatnik look. "Maybe she doesn't want whoever it is to know her cell number. Some people don't like their number to get spread around."

"Maybe," Ginger said, her mind already distracted from the habits of her guest as she looked down at the pink message slips. "She is French, after all."

"So?"

"Ever been to Martinique?"

"Right." Jules grinned. "*Do not bother me simply because you are a guest spending your money in my place of business and you have been waiting for your drink order for thirty minutes. You do not speak French and are therefore beneath my contempt. And when I finally condescend to bring you the wrong order, I will run after you and curse you in French for not leaving a tip.*" Jules' accent and tone were dead on the money.

Ginger laughed. "Exactly. But be nice to her if you want a paycheck this week."

"You should have charged those jerks for the days remaining on their reservations. It's not like they're in danger from ghosts or anything."

"They were within their rights to check out early. It isn't every day you go on vacation and wake up to a dead body in the room next door. Besides, I can't afford to have bad reviews popping up on travel websites. Let's just hope none of them decide to share their 'harrowing, near-death experience' on line."

"How bad are things?" Jules looked truly alarmed.

Ginger smiled at his expression and shook her head. "Not that bad, for Pete's sake. But it would be nice to do more than break even. I'm trying to finish the reno on the garage apartment and I'd like to get it done this year. It would help with taxes, among other things."

"I don't need to be polishing off my resumé, then?"

"Nope. I'm going to fix something to eat. You want anything?"

"I can always eat."

"Okay." Ginger stuffed the messages into her pocket. "I'll see what's in the fridge."

The cat was ahead of her, waiting impatiently in the doorway to the kitchen. "I think Trouble's hungry," she said as she crossed the foyer.

"Cats," Jules said. "There were two from the Hemingway house out by the back patio earlier this evening. I thought they were supposed to be locked up at night."

Trouble pricked his ears forward then zoomed through the door to the dining room and the kitchen beyond. He was out of sight in a flash.

"They're harmless," Ginger said. "It's just some dumb government regulation. No one pays any attention to it anymore."

When Ginger entered the kitchen, Trouble was pacing by the back door. "Yeow," he complained. "Yeow."

"What? We were just outside. Aren't you hungry?"

Trouble scratched at the door.

"Fine." Ginger crossed the kitchen and opened the door. The cat took off and disappeared into the low lighting of the back garden of the Paradise. "Crazy cat," she said. She started to turn back into the kitchen then thought better of it. What if he wandered off? If there were other cats on the grounds, would he stray with them? Tammy would kill her if something happened to Trouble.

She went onto the back porch and called his name. Not a leaf rustled in the deep foliage. "Great." Ginger set off along the pathway that wound through the back garden. After a thorough search, she gave up. Trouble was nowhere to be found, not hiding under the lounge chairs by the pool, or anywhere near the tiki bar. She pondered what to do then decided the best way to a cat's heart was the same as a man's. Food. When she entered the kitchen, she left the back door open just enough for him to squeeze through. Tonight's menu would definitely be fish.

TROUT WAS FINISHING his second beer when he decided he should have taken Ginger up on her invitation. She never told him how she knew about his encounter with Liberty. How could she have known, he wondered. Maybe the detective told her after all. Now he looked guilty in her eyes and that bothered him more than the suspicions of the police.

He debated opening a third beer but thought better of it. He hadn't eaten anything since the blueberry muffin and coffee at the Paradise. The wisest course would be to get something to eat. A perusal of his pantry and refrigerator produced nothing but beer, a rotting tomato, some iffy yogurt, and dried pasta. He was light in the pockets but he decided he could just manage a meal at the Smokin' Tuna. Maybe Ginger hadn't started cooking dinner yet. Maybe she would want to join him. Maybe not. He took another beer from the mini fridge and popped the top. He wasn't really that hungry.

CHAPTER THREE

*a*ll of Megs and Bartholomew's ramblings about secret agents and court orders now makes some sense. At least it's not so stream of consciousness now that I have an inkling of the underlying issue. The question is, do they perceive a real threat from discovery in their wanderings, or is what Ginger said the truth of the matter, that no one is concerned about enforcing the restrictions on the Hemingway cats. I cannot see how this could play into the murder of Liberty Anderson but a good detective leaves no stone unturned.

First, I'll check the little fire escape landing on the east side of the house. I get the impression it's a favorite spot for Megs and Bartholomew. Now, as I see it at night, I realize it's quite a good vantage point for two-thirds of the grounds of the Paradise.

The pool glimmers with underwater lights. It's a small pool, more for cooling off from the summer heat, I should think, than actually swimming. Still, I guess it allows Ginger to advertise it as an amenity.

No one is sitting at the al fresco tables or on the stools at the tiki bar. With only two of the seven rooms of the bed and breakfast occupied, I can understand why. Mademoiselle Benoit has gone out for the evening. I'm not sure about the Talents.

If only I could figure out how to get onto the gallery that runs along the front of the main building I could discover if they're in their room. I could also learn if that's how the killer gained access to Liberty's room. I see no easy way to scale the side of the building. There isn't even a trellis for roses or whatever blooming thing that grows out of control here in the tropics.

The fire escape window is secure from access from the outside, that I know. One of the policemen checked the internal locking mechanism this morning. There's no evidence it has been tampered with from the outside. Even if it had, the killer would still need to gain entry into Liberty's room. A room that was most assuredly locked from the inside this morning.

There's no sign of life on the grounds of the property except for Ginger who is intent on finding me. As soon as she returns to the kitchen I'll hustle down the stairs and go to the Hemingway House. If Megs and Bartholomew aren't here, then surely they're there.

GINGER SEALED the container of fresh cut fruit for the next morning's breakfast and stored it in the enormous refrigerator. She loaded the coffeemaker and set out clean cups and saucers, spoons, a variety of sweeteners, and a stack of bread and butter plates for pastries.

She picked up Trouble's plate of sautéed trigger fish with butter and capers sauce and covered it with wrap. She hoped he showed up before she closed up for the night. With everything else that was going on right now, the last thing she needed was a lost cat, Tammy Lynn's lost cat.

She expelled a soul deep sigh. Finding him on an island crawling with cats would take a major stroke of luck and be darn near impossible. She kept reminding herself that Tammy Lynn said he was smarter than the average cat. All she could do was hope that meant he could find his way back to the Paradise when he got hungry enough.

Half way through dinner with Jules she had also remembered that the Flamenco Suite still hadn't been made up. It was tempting to leave it until morning but she knew that was a sure path to chaos. A convention was arriving in town on Wednesday and she would be totally booked. It was best to stay on top of things when she had the time. The energy to do so was another story, but it had to be done. She would put a call in to Gabriella tomorrow to be sure she could help fill in for the duration of the full house.

As she finally closed the door on the clean and tidy Flamenco Suite, Ginger rubbed the ache in the back of her neck. She looked at the hallway clock. Eleven forty-five. When she reached the foot of the stairs she glanced at the partially closed door to the office cubby behind the registration counter. Jules was propped up on the daybed, his book lying open across his chest, and his head back against the pillows in sleep.

She had heard the Talents come in while she was making the bed in the Flamenco Suite. They were a cute couple celebrating their first wedding anniversary. Most of their time was spent holed up in the Macaw Suite but they made occasional forays into the night life of Key West. Young love, Ginger thought and smiled.

The key board at the front desk showed Annette Benoit's key still on the hook. Ginger frowned and shook her head. It would be nice to have everyone in and accounted for before she called it a day but that was rarely the case. People came to Key West to enjoy themselves and more often than not that meant partaking of the legendary night life.

She switched the front door of the Paradise to auto lock

and dimmed the porch lights. A swipe pad would allow her errant guest to gain entry when she returned. In the event a guest was too intoxicated or couldn't find their key card, there was a buzzer that would rouse Jules.

It had been a long day and she was ready to hit the sack. As she crossed the foyer to the hallway leading to her private rooms, she heard a muffled thump from upstairs. Trouble, she thought. He must have come in while she was in the Flamenco Suite. The crazy cat was obsessed with the Toucan Suite, had been even before they found Liberty's dead body.

She went back up the curving staircase and turned in the direction of the noise she had heard. Out of the dim light of the wall sconces, a dark image sprang up from the door lock of the Toucan Suite and slammed into her, knocking her against the landing banister where she hit her head on the newel post. The intruder streaked past her and was headed down the stairs before Ginger's body hit the floor. She felt a sharp pain near her temple and knew she was losing consciousness.

TROUT SAT for an hour or more vacillating on the merits of breaking into his contingency fund. It was a hard call, one he had determined he wouldn't make except in dire circumstances. Then he thought about Liberty Anderson, dead while on holiday in paradise, and decided life was short.

He opened the locked cabinet under the banquet and took out a once expensive but now battered leather wallet. It contained ten one-hundred-dollar bills. He paused, fingering the bills, then took one and slipped it into his pocket before leaving the dock in search of food.

He sat at the bar and ate the plate of fish tacos the Smokin' Tuna was known for and washed them down with his fourth beer of the evening. The night crowd was changing. Tourists were giving way to locals as the hour grew late. He debated whether or not to have another beer but decided he'd better not.

At some point in the past year and a half he had started counting when he started drinking. It was his own method of self-regulation. There were days when he didn't drink anything. Sometimes those days would turn into a string that didn't end for a couple of weeks or more. Three beers were a bad day, he decided. A six pack was a really crappy day. He was once again being tempted by the thought of a fifth beer when the detective Ginger called Duncan waltzed in off the street to the outdoor bar at the Smokin' Tuna.

This was turning into a really crappy day, Trout decided. Duncan zeroed in on him and crossed the open patio to take the stool next to his.

"Been looking for you," Duncan said.

"Why's that?"

"You're an interesting guy, Armentrout Richardson." Duncan motioned for the bartender as he spoke. When she leaned across to him, he ordered a vodka tonic.

Trout waited. He knew the policeman would get to the point in his own good time. There was always a point to be made in these situations, he thought.

"A charter boat captain is a big career change for a man like you, don't you think?"

"How so?"

Duncan shrugged in that funny way he had. "All that education, white collar job, soft hands. Seems to me like a big change."

"If you're going to make a change, it might as well be a big one."

"I suppose." Duncan took a sip of his drink. "I imagine you had more than enough reason." He looked at Trout. "The suicide and all. Wait. Not one suicide but two, isn't that right?"

"What is it you really want to say, detective?"

"I like Ginger. She's good people."

"I like her, too."

"I don't think you're hearing me." Duncan banged his glass down on the bar. "I think you spell trouble and Ginger doesn't need any more crap in her life."

"Two things." Trout stood, took the hundred-dollar bill from his pocket, and signaled for his check. "First, I hardly know Ginger and therefore am not an issue in her life one way or the other." The bartender made change for him. "And second." He left a tip and crammed the rest of the money into his pocket. "I like to eat alone." He turned and headed toward the exit.

Duncan's phone rang on Trout's parting shot and he answered with a clipped, "Yes." After a split second he said, "What?" He was already moving past Trout to the street. "How bad is she?" He opened the door of a double parked unmarked sedan on the street in front of the Smokin' Tuna. "Lock down the Paradise. Don't let so much as a mouse in or out until I get there."

Trout caught the door of the car as Duncan tried to close it. "It's Ginger, isn't it?"

Duncan jerked the door closed as he started the car. He tore away from the curb on squealing tires.

Trout started to run. It was three blocks to Petronia Street. He reached the Paradise just minutes after Duncan.

I CAN'T BELIEVE I *didn't see this coming. Clearly whoever killed*

Liberty didn't get what he was after. This is his handiwork. I know it in my bones. His scent still lingers though it is growing faint.

It grieves me to return to the Paradise and this, the back door open, Jules asleep on the job, and Ginger badly wounded. I don't know how long she's been out but thank heavens she's coming around. At least Jules isn't a heavy sleeper. He came the instant I called out and has been on the phone with emergency services and the police.

Ginger groans and holds her head. Jules is back at her side.

"Don't move, Ginger. The paramedics are on the way."

"I'm okay..." she tries to rise then slumps back onto the carpet runner of the upper landing and groans again. "My head."

The police are banging at the door and Jules runs down the stairs to trip the lock and let them in. Paramedics are on their heels, medical cases in hand. I heave a sigh of relief. Tammy will be so upset if I've let her friend come to any real harm.

The Talents come out of their room swaddled in bath robes. A policeman shoos them back inside and asks them to wait until they have control of the situation. I foresee another departure from the Paradise come morning.

The paramedics have barely begun to minister to Ginger's wound when Detective Moore appears on the scene. His face is white with concern or rage, I'm not sure which at this point. He kneels beside her and pushes her hair from her face.

"Hey, kiddo. What's going on?"

She smiles then winces. "I'm not sure. I heard a noise and came upstairs. I thought it was the cat." She closes her eyes.

"Ginger?" Duncan's voice is sharp.

The paramedic pushes him aside. He forces Ginger's eye open and checks it with a penlight.

"Stop." Ginger whispers as she turns her head to the side, away from the probing light. "I'm okay." She licks her lips. "It hurts to talk."

"Get her to the hospital," Duncan says.

Ginger grabs his arm. "No. I need to be here."

"You've got a head injury. Don't argue."

"The Paradise..."

"Jules can take care of things."

Tears begin to seep from beneath Ginger's closed eyelids. "Please, Duncan."

"Crap," he says under his breath. "Don't do that, Ginger. Just get a CT scan. If things are okay you can come back home."

"I'll stay, Ginger." Trout is standing over the men kneeling around Ginger. He's breathing heavily.

She opens her eyes, then closes them and gives a faint nod.

The coppers have the situation with Ginger in hand. I need to investigate before they turn their minds to the actual crime scene and start mucking about in things. The door of the Toucan Suite is closed. I can't say whether or not it's still locked. If only I had an opposable thumb. Where are Megs and Bartholomew when they might actually be of help? Oh, well, I'm sure this will be determined by the bipeds before much longer.

I trot down the hallway and around the corner past the Bird Cage and linen closet to the emergency exit window. Its lock is still secure. That means nothing, of course, as it automatically locks when closed. Still, I know our intruder didn't enter this way or it would be broken. I don't think our culprit left this way either. There is an absence of the scent that hovered on the landing when I first arrived from my search for Megs and Bartholomew. Obviously, the back door is the point of entry and escape. If only I hadn't dallied at the Hemingway House none of this would have happened.

Downstairs I find the door to Ginger's quarters is ajar. The murderer's scent is here. My blood boils with the realization that he violated her sanctuary. If she had been in her room the circumstances might be much worse than they are.

Our killer is definitely looking for something. He has been through

Ginger's desk. It was a tidy job, but very thorough. The good news is that he didn't recognize Liberty Anderson's cell phone. It sits smack in the middle of the desktop where Ginger left it. Why would he overlook it?

It's obvious Ginger is still laboring under the delusion that Liberty's death is from some as yet unknown medical cause or a result of self-inflicted alcohol poisoning. Otherwise she would have put the phone in a secure place. But even I didn't anticipate the return of our miscreant.

Whatever the reason he didn't take the phone, I'm not one to leave any source of possible clues unchecked. I feel a pressing need to gain access to whatever information it holds, but how? I will leave it for now. Best to check the exterior of the Paradise to see if our marauder left any evidence behind.

I say, what's this? It appears our villain waited for his opportunity behind the tiki hut. The shutters are askew. It's a good spot from which to monitor the activities of the bed and breakfast. It's even better that the two cabins back here are unoccupied at the moment.

From this vantage point the intruder is assured privacy and you can just see down the side of the building to the steps leading onto the front porch. Anyone coming or going would be noticed. The whole of the backside of the Paradise is visible, the kitchen on full display through the undraped window. He had an unobstructed view of the dining room through the bay window and of Ginger's quarters, fortuitously lit from within by a desk lamp. All the villain had to do was wait and watch.

A rustling sounds from the bed of cast iron plants and I crouch, ready to spring. It is only Megs and Bartholomew.

"Where have you been?" I ask.

"Here and there," Bartholomew answers.

"Doing what?"

"This and that." He's momentarily distracted by a moth.

"No one saw us," Megs says.

"Saw you doing what?"

She doesn't answer my question, instead she sidles up beside me, purrs, and bats her eyelashes. "Whatcha doin' out here, Trouble?"

"Looking for a killer."

"The one with the strange smell?" She nuzzles my ear.

I twitch my ears and shake my head as I back away. "You've seen him?"

Bartholomew clears his throat, "Seen who? Neither saw nor been seen. Not me, not Megs."

"Enough!" I say. "This is serious business. A woman was killed last night."

"The spy." Megs nods her head. "It was bound to happen."

I have had enough of this cat and mouse game with Bartholomew and Megs. Either they've eaten too much mercury-laced tuna or they think they're penning a literary tale of the Alice in Wonderland variety. I shall have some straight answers out of these two before the sun rises. It's time to charm the truth out of Megs if I can get past the thought of her strange crossed eyes. The polydactyl business doesn't help matters. Six toes are an aberration but seven? What's a cat supposed to do with all those toes, anyway?

THE POLICE DIDN'T clear out of the bed and breakfast until well after two in the morning. The black cat kept pace with Trout as he locked the front door behind the last of them and checked that the kitchen door was also secure. He took a stance in front of an empty bowl on the floor near the pantry and began to complain. Trout got the message and opened the large refrigerator. He spied the covered container of fish with some kind of sauce.

"Now I really am sorry I missed dinner," he said to the cat as he unwrapped the contents of the dish and slid it into Trouble's bowl. "I bet you'd like some water as well." Trouble didn't pause from his repast to comment. Trout grinned and took the bowl marked water and filled it.

Once the cat finished eating, he looked up at Trout as he ran his tongue over his mouth and cleaned his whiskers. "What?" Trout asked. "In or out? Is that it?"

"Yeow," the cat said and took off across the kitchen to the hallway and then to the back of the bed and breakfast. He stopped and looked back at Trout when he came to a closed door at the end of the hall.

Trout watched him and the cat did the darnedest thing. He stretched up to the door knob with his forepaws and scratched at it.

"What's this about?" He asked as he opened the door. Immediately he knew he was in Ginger's private quarters. When he would step back into the hall the cat streaked in and hopped onto the desk.

"Yeow," he said and with a flick of his paw sent a cell phone in the center of the desk spinning to the floor.

Trout retrieved the phone and when he replaced it on the desk, the cat yowled again.

"What's with you, crazy cat?" Trout tried to pick Trouble up to take him from the room and the cat hissed and bowed his back.

Once again, Trouble's paw whipped out and sent the phone flying across the room.

Trout looked from the cat to the phone. This time when he picked it up, he pushed the button and activated it. He wasn't sure what he was supposed to do but he felt certain the cat wanted him to do something. He felt a little ridiculous doing the cat's bidding but he clicked on the call log anyway. It showed a bunch of numbers from a 202 area code. Trout knew that code from his former career as a psychologist for DCF. It was Washington, DC. He looked at the messages, reading the script of the last one. It was then he realized this wasn't Ginger's phone. It belonged to Liberty.

The last message she received prompted him to open Liberty's Facebook page. Like Ginger had before him, he went to her camera feature as well. So, this was how Ginger had known he met Liberty before her death.

Trout sat at the desk and stared at the iPhone. It would be a simple thing to delete the photo. No one would be the wiser. Except Ginger. The question was, why did Ginger have Liberty's phone? Surely the police would have taken it with them when they came to investigate her death. Something was nagging at him about the why and how of this situation.

He scrolled back through the photographs more slowly trying to see if there was something in one of them that he had missed. As he flicked from one to another, Trouble suddenly put his paw on the screen of the phone.

Trout moved the phone from the cat's reach and looked at the photo. It was of a man holding a gray and white cat. The man had looked away from the photographer and only a little of his profile and horn-rimmed glasses were visible.

"Is this one of your friends?" he asked Trouble.

"Yeow." Trouble said.

Trout scratched him behind his ears. "It looks like the little one from the back yard."

"Yeow."

He glanced at the clock on the bedside radio. Nearly three in the morning. He was tired, his brain wasn't functioning as it should. What he needed was sleep but he had promised Ginger he would man the fort until she returned from the hospital. Jules was upset, blaming himself for the break-in.

Maybe he could say something to make him feel better, Trout thought, and closed the door on Ginger's room, a struggling black cat in his arms.

GINGER TURNED toward the sound of the hospital door opening. Duncan put his head around it and said, "Hey, you decent?"

"Yes. Come in. What did you find?"

He rolled his shoulders in a shrug. "Nothing so far. I can't tell if he was trying to pick the lock on the murder room or not until you have a look see. It could be that all those scratches are from former guests having issues with sobriety."

"Could be," she said. "You said murder room?"

"It looks that way. At the very least, manslaughter. Her alcohol level was point two one eight but the urine test also showed GHB. A deadly combination. She was purposely drugged somewhere along her route of partying night before last. Clearly there was intent to at least immobilize her."

"How could she make it back to her room if she was drugged?"

"It takes twenty minutes to an hour for a roofie to fully kick in. The problem is the time of death. She wasn't at the Paradise at one o'clock, that we know. Obviously, she came in at some point afterwards. The room was air conditioned so the ME has to take that into consideration. Also, how long it took her to die. No way to determine that with any certainty."

"So, it was date rape?"

"Looks that way on the face of it but there's no evidence of sexual activity. Whoever it was must have gotten scared off or lost his nerve. Maybe he was afraid of getting caught coming or going from an establishment as small as the Paradise. Who knows."

Ginger knew she shouldn't feel such a sense of relief but she did. Liberty's death was because she crossed paths with the wrong person. It didn't make the taint go away completely but as far as publicity went, the same thing could have happened if she'd been staying at any other accommodation in Key West.

Her death had already made the local morning news coverage. No doubt there would be a write up in the *Key West Citizen*. If Ginger was lucky, the *Miami Herald* wouldn't pick up the story. She adjusted her position in the hospital bed and winced.

"You okay?" Duncan asked.

"Fine." She lightly touched the bandage on her head. Something was floating at the edge of her memory but she could quite grasp it.

"What did the doc say about the crack on the head?"

"I'll live."

"I need a little more than that, Ginger."

"Some swelling, no intracranial bleeding, a few stitches. Nothing that won't right itself in a couple of days. The good news is that the paramedics packed my head with ice to keep the swelling at a minimum. Remind me to bake them a key lime pie."

"No bleeding, huh?"

"Nothing to worry about. Dr. Harrison says the body will take care of itself. I have a very hard head."

"True."

She laughed then grimaced. "Stop. I want to get out of here this afternoon."

"What time?"

"He said around one if I behave."

"I'll swing by and get you."

"You don't need to do that."

"Apparently, I do. Someone has to keep you out of trouble. Besides, you can take a look at the lock on the Toucan Suite and give me your opinion. See if anything else looks out of place, tell me if the tape was still intact the last time you noticed."

Ginger blushed crimson. "Oh. About that."

Duncan's brows shot up in a knowing look. "About that, what?"

"The tape. I cut it."

He said nothing for a long tick of the clock. "Why?"

"The phone. I could hear the phone ringing and, well, I went in to answer it."

When she said nothing else, he asked, "Don't keep me in suspense. Who was it?"

"I don't know. I mean, I do, and I don't. The phone quit ringing as soon as I opened the door."

"So, explain to me how you do and you don't know who was calling."

"The call log. On her cell phone."

"You have her cell phone?"

"That's what I said."

"I thought you meant the room phone."

"Oh." Ginger could see his temper rising. She hoped his wrath would be directed toward the underling who failed to find the iPhone when they searched Liberty's room. "It was under the dressing table. It must have fallen out of her purse."

"So, that's what he was after."

It took a second for Ginger to realize the implication of Duncan's comment and she understood why he was being so protective. Why the killer had returned to the Paradise hadn't been resolved to Duncan's satisfaction. Now there was a reason; to find Liberty's cell phone. His photograph must be among the party photos. What other explanation could there be? Then she remembered that Trout's picture was also on Liberty's phone.

CHAPTER FOUR

*I*t's sometimes a chore to work with bipeds. They haven't the facile skills of detection that come naturally to me. It's often like their expression 'pulling teeth' to steer them where they need to go. Ah, well, I must work with what I have. Right now, I need to get into the locked Toucan Suite. Ginger is safely home and she and Duncan have brought Trout into their line of thought as to why Liberty died. I must make them understand that it's a false premise. Something more is going on here and right now I don't have a clue as to what.

Detective Moore has Liberty's cell phone. His hostility toward Trout is not helped by what he sees there.

"This was what time?"

Trout shrugs. "Eleven or so. I'm sure you have someone who can determine when the picture was taken. And you can ask Evan. He was tending bar. He'll probably remember. Approximately."

"This little party you mentioned, the one that was headed out to The Oriole, how do I know you didn't go with them?"

"You'll just have to take my word for it, I guess. And it wasn't a party headed that way, more like she was trying to talk it up."

Duncan grunts. He doesn't give the impression of someone willing *to take Trout's word for anything.*

"You knew this picture was on her phone?"

"Honestly, I didn't think about it. We crossed paths like people do in a bar. She stood out because she wanted to be noticed. At least that's the impression I got."

"That's your professional opinion, I take it," Duncan says, "as a psychologist."

Trout glances at Ginger then looks Duncan square in the eyes. "I observe people, form opinions, same as anyone else."

"Except you have a bunch of letters after your name that say you analyze people, see the patterns in their actions, predict their behavior."

Trout clinches his jaw then releases it. "No one can predict how any given individual will react to life's challenges. You simply work with them to get to the core of their pain, teach them options, coping mechanisms."

"Uh huh."

Ginger stirs on the sofa in the informal sitting room where she's lying. "Won't the pictures help you retrace her steps from last night?"

Ah, Ginger once again comes to Trout's rescue, distracting the detective from him. It is as I suspected, the heart trumps the head.

Duncan glances at Ginger. I can see he's drawing the same conclusion.

"Sure," he says as he slips Liberty's phone into his coat pocket. "We already have her credit card charges. This will help us recreate a timeline and start taking statements from anyone who might have seen her. We might even get lucky and find out if anyone was paying her particular attention. So far, we've had no luck reaching anyone at her home in Virginia. The local cops are going to check out the address for us. Maybe her boss can shed a little light on things. Now that I know about her boss."

Ginger blushes.

"You got a quiet spot where I can make some calls?" he asks.

"The desk in my quarters. There's a laptop as well if you need it." Ginger sits up and swings her feet to the floor.

"I can do what I need to with my phone. And you're supposed to be on bed rest."

"There's too much to do. There's a convention on Wednesday..."

"Forty-eight hours. Doctor's orders." Duncan motions his head in Trout's direction. *"The shrink will see to the Paradise."*

Trout crosses the room to Ginger. *"Stop worrying. Jules and I have everything under control. We got breakfast with what was already in the refrigerator and the bread basket. It was easy enough. Only the Talents came down. They've been given vouchers to the Smokin' Tuna for dinner as a good will gesture. Gabriella is cleaning their room as we speak."* He helps Ginger to stand and turns her toward the back of the building. *"Everything's going to be fine but only if you allow yourself to mend."*

Well, that worry is off my plate. As long as Duncan and Trout are sparring over Ginger I know she'll get the care she needs. Trout seems to be getting through to her. A nice lie down will do wonders for her. She's still quite pale.

Duncan heads for the empty dining room, his cell phone in one hand and Liberty's cell phone in the other. I'll just check that Ginger's room is secure then I'll see if I can prompt Trout to open the Toucan Suite.

The police are operating under the impression that the killer wasn't in Liberty's room, that she came back to the bed and breakfast alone and locked herself in. But I know better. The killer was in there. The question is whether or not he was in there when Liberty died.

I need to make them realize that even though the room was locked, he managed to gain access somehow. And I need to find whatever he was searching for. That's the key to this case. Once we know the what, we'll be able to determine the why, and track down the who.

. . .

TROUT SENT Jules home as soon as he settled Ginger in her bed and Duncan cleared out, talking on his cell phone the whole while.

Annette Benoit came breezing into the foyer. It was after two in the afternoon and Trout realized she had been out all night and most of the day. She had that elegantly disheveled look that many strive for but French women so easily affect. Not my business, he thought. She collected the key to the Bird Cage and swept up the stairs past the cat.

Trouble had been restless and vocal since Duncan's departure from the Paradise. Food wasn't the answer and he didn't want to go out. He kept returning to the third step of the stairs leading up to the second floor, waiting but not very patiently. Trout tried to ignore him but the cat wasn't having it.

Trout listened to the sounds of Angela and Gabriella as they prepared the dining room for breakfast the next day. The murmur of their conversation and the clink of china and silverware created no demands on his concentration as his mind worried at the tangle of events swirling around the Paradise. His gaze settled on the cat.

"Yeow."

Trout noted that he tended to favor the third step of the stairs. Black cats, a sudden death, numerology. He laughed at the direction his thoughts were taking. He got up from the stool behind the reception desk and turned down the hallway to Ginger's quarters to check on her.

It wasn't really a surprise to find her sitting at her dressing table examining the gash on her head. "You were meant to be resting."

"Can't sleep. Never have been one to nap during the day. Besides, all the medications they gave me in the wee hours this morning have worn off and I'm wide awake."

"How are you feeling?"

"Fine. A bit of a headache still but that's all."

"No blurry vision, dizziness?"

"Honestly. Between you and Duncan you'd think I was an invalid." Ginger stood and turned from addressing his image in the mirror of her dressing table to the real thing. "Mainly I feel ticked off that someone thinks they can run amuck at the Paradise, bashing people in the head, trespassing..." She paused. "That poor woman."

"Yeah." Trout jangled the change in his pocket. "How about a cup of coffee?"

"Maybe some tea?"

"Sure." He gave Ginger one last assessing look and turned from the room.

Duncan and Ginger seemed convinced that the murderer had returned to the Paradise because he feared his image was on Liberty's phone. It sounded logical, it certainly fit the facts. Yet something about the whole thing bothered Trout. Something he couldn't put his finger on. He shook his head.

When Ginger entered the kitchen, Trout noticed she had brushed her hair. The way it formed a wave of curls over the right side of her forehead hid the stitches. She looked good for someone who had been knocked unconscious a mere sixteen hours earlier. But then, she always looked good to him. He knew the floral print wrap skirts and sleeveless white shirts she wore were her concession to a professional uniform as the owner of the B & B but they sure looked sexy on her.

He placed the steaming cup of tea and a plate of cookies in front of where she sat at the long kitchen work table. For himself he poured a cup of the coffee Angela had made to go with the afternoon cookies.

The cat came in from the lobby and began to complain to Ginger.

She reached down and scratched him under the chin. "What do you want? Are you hungry?"

"He's not hungry. He doesn't want to go out. He has plenty of water. He's just being a pain in the butt."

"Did you feed him?"

"Scrambled eggs with goat cheese and heavy cream."

"Wow." Ginger took a sip of her tea. "No one ever spoiled me like that."

"I couldn't find any cat food."

"Trouble doesn't eat cat food. He has a very discerning palate. He should be your best buddy after that feast."

"Well, there's no pleasing him. I thought cats slept twenty-three hours a day."

"That's dogs. He just wants to get into the Toucan Suite."

"How do you know?"

"I speak cat."

"Ha ha." Trout took one of the sugar cookies from Ginger's plate. "So, tell me about Duncan."

"What about him?"

Trout noticed that the question brought a spot of color to Ginger's cheeks. "You two seem to know each other pretty well."

"We're both conchs, born on the island, always lived on the island except for about six years for me. We've known each other all our lives, went to school together. He's a friend."

"It seems like more."

Ginger turned the tea cup around and around on the table top. She sighed. "It was for a while. A very short while. And it was a mistake. Now we're just trying to be what we once were, friends."

She stopped turning the cup and looked up at Trout. "A psychologist, huh?"

"For a while. A long while, actually. It was a mistake. Now I'm a charter boat captain."

"Seems like there's more to it than that."

When Trout didn't say anything Ginger waited.

Finally, he said, "I worked for the state, DCF. In Tallahassee. My patients were the runaways, the throwaways, and the forgotten." He stood and emptied his cup of cold coffee in the sink. "There aren't a lot of success stories in that line of work. After a while you're either just going through the motions or it grinds you down."

The cat was once again under his feet, making a figure eight between his legs. "Yeow."

"What?"

Ginger stood and brought her tea cup to the sink. "I think we should see what's in the Toucan Suite."

THE TOUCAN SUITE held the scent of abandonment, Ginger thought as she opened the door. It had only been vacant one day yet it seemed so void of life, as if it had been empty for a long time. Perhaps that's what sudden death does to a space, she thought.

Trout used the toe of his tennis shoe to swing the door to the bathroom open. "When did they say you could clean the room?"

"They, meaning Duncan, didn't say. I'll have to give him a call and ask. I have a reservation for this room in three days."

"She was leaving in three days?"

"She was leaving tomorrow." Ginger decided to follow Trout's example. She took a tissue from the dispenser on the dressing table and used it to safeguard against leaving any prints and opened the armoire.

Something about the decision to take such precautions made her heartbeat accelerate. There was no reason for it to do so, she told herself. The mystery of Liberty's death had been resolved. She died from a combination of alcohol and drugs. End of story. This was a room in the Paradise, her bed and breakfast. Decades of polishing this furniture, cleaning this bathroom, checking the armoire and the highboy for forgotten items through the years of ownership by her grandmother, her mother, and now herself, made it as familiar to her as her own rooms.

"You okay?"

Trout's question, spoken so near, made her jump. He had moved from a perusal of the bathroom to her side without her realizing it.

"Sorry. Didn't mean to spook you."

She tried for a smile. "I'm being silly. I guess it's the idea that someone died at the Paradise, right here in this room."

"A natural reaction. Anyone else ever die here?"

"My grandmother when I was nine. And my mother four years ago but I wasn't here at the time. Other than that I don't know. Logic would suggest that there have been deaths here over the long history of the house but none that I'm aware of."

He nodded and turned his attention to Trouble who crawled out from under the bed and sat on his haunches and stared into space. "Looks like he didn't find what he wanted," Trout said.

"He does seem disappointed."

Trout moved to the floor-to-ceiling windows on the far side of the room. The furniture arrangement created a path to one of them so guests would have easy access to the gallery. He checked that it was locked, then unlocked it and raised it. It gave a familiar low squeal as the hidden pulley weights lowered to raise the sash.

Trout stepped out onto the gallery. The cat followed him, sniffing the threshold and the immediate area of the wide covered space. Once again Trouble sat and stared out into the distance. Ginger watched both cat and man for several seconds. Both seemed lost in thought. She stepped through the window and joined them.

Trout stood near the railing, his hands in his pockets, and seemed miles away. Trouble glanced at Ginger then walked along the gallery investigating each window that opened onto it. Three rooms of the Paradise had access to this inviting space in the same manner as the Toucan Suite. The middle room, the Flamenco Suite, was vacant, the occupants having been the first to depart in the wake of Liberty's death. The Talents occupied the Macaw Suite, the last of the rooms that could be accessed from this gallery.

Ginger settled into one of the outdoor chaise lounges and closed her eyes. The deep shade of the roof overhang made this a perfect idyll for guests willing to pay the higher rate for one of these rooms. She listened to the sound of tourists passing along the street below as they debated what to see next. The faint skittering of claws alerted her that Eddie the iguana had appeared on the scene, checking to see who had invaded his aerie. A sense of calm spread over her and for the first time in two days she began to relax.

When Ginger opened her eyes, she realized the day was fading. She turned to see Trout in the chaise lounge beside her, Trouble curled at his feet. She pushed herself into a more upright position.

"Sorry. I must have dozed off."

"You needed the rest."

"Have you been here the whole while?"

"Pretty much. I went down to talk to Angela. She's manning the front desk."

"Thanks."

"I've been thinking."

"About?"

"You remember telling me you caught a scent of something in Liberty's room?"

Ginger stretched her arms over her head and stifled a yawn. "It had a sweetness to it."

"Huh." Trout grew quiet for several seconds. "Have you ever smelled it before?"

"I'm not sure. At the time, it seemed familiar but I couldn't place it. I wasn't even sure I'd smelled anything after that first instant when I opened the door. It was such a fleeting sensation."

"But it was something you thought to be out of the ordinary for a woman's room?"

"I guess." Ginger swung her legs over the side of the chaise lounge and stood. "Why?"

Trout unfolded his long frame from the other lounger and stood also, disturbing Trouble in the process. "I don't know. Something feels off. I can't put my finger on it."

Ginger felt a thread of apprehension creep along her spine at his words. She rubbed her arms against a non-existent chill in the late August afternoon. "Let's hope not. I don't need any more trouble."

"Right."

They stepped back through the tall window opening into the Toucan Suite. Trout closed and locked it. Ginger didn't linger in the room. As soon as Trout and Trouble came through the door into the hallway she started to pull it closed. Her eyes skimmed over the room one last time and stopped at the high-boy. Sitting atop it was something that didn't belong there.

At last Trout has seen the light. Or at least begun to listen to his instincts. Neither he nor Ginger have been quick off the mark on this case but then they are merely bipeds. I've been frustrated by my inability to communicate with him. He didn't understand my interest in the photo on Liberty's phone and there's no way I can make him see that a photo of Megs holds little interest for me. I do believe, however, things are looking up with Ginger. Something has caught her eye.

"Trout," *she pushes the door wide and steps back into the Toucan Suite.*

He turns at the odd sound of her voice and joins her. "What?"

"There. On top of the highboy. That doesn't belong in this room."

"Where does it belong?"

"I don't know. I've never seen it before."

All three of us stare at the silk covered rectangular box atop the highboy. The design is Asian. An ivory toggle serves to fasten it. After a second's pause, Trout reaches up and brings down the box that looks to be about fifteen by twenty-five centimeters.

"It's heavy," *Trout says.*

Ginger eyes the elaborately decorated container but doesn't touch it. "It must belong to Liberty."

Trout places it on the dressing table. "This could be what the killer was after."

Ginger looks from the box to Trout and back. "We should call Duncan."

Neither of them makes a move to put her words into action. Now we're getting somewhere. If they'll only open the box. I jump onto the dressing table and sniff at it. "Yeow." *There is no trace of the murderer's scent on the box which tells me he overlooked it. That makes me think he didn't recognize it as the object he sought. If it actually is what he was after. Surely it must be.*

"Yeow."

"Get down, Trouble." Ginger lifts me and deposits me on the floor. "This is evidence."

I couldn't agree more but unless we open it, we won't know the motive for the crime. Detective Moore's concern for Ginger has raised my opinion of him but not so much his sleuthing skills. I must press the point if we are to make any progress. I jump back onto the dressing table.

Trout grabs me and puts me out the door then closes it. I can't believe it! Doesn't he understand what's at stake? This is worse than Megs' description of the perp as a thin man with a lovely voice wearing a Hawaiian print shirt. Every other tourist in Key West is wearing a Hawaiian print shirt though the descriptive 'thin' does narrow the field considerably among today's American males. She did say the man's scent reminded her of Papa Hemingway. Another of her delusions and a dead end if there ever was one. Even with nine lives she couldn't have known Hemingway considering the fact that he killed himself in 1961. Are we to believe the murderer is a ghost? Nonsense.

"WE SHOULD OPEN IT," Trout said. "This might be the reason someone wanted to drug her."

"The police think Liberty was the target of date rape."

"So, no harm no foul."

"If this is the reason Liberty died, we'd be tampering with evidence."

"We're not tampering with anything. The police left this along with the clothes in the armoire, Liberty's suitcase, and several pair of shoes. They didn't see any reason to process them as evidence."

"This is different," Ginger said. "They looked through all her belongings and only took what they thought might have some bearing on what happened to her, her purse and its contents, her make-up. They were looking for an overdose or something that could be a source of poison. They even took her laptop to see if anything on it could suggest a motive." She worried her lower lip as she stared at the box that seemed to scream trouble. "No one would think this belonged to a guest. It looks like a purposeful decoration, something meant to be part of the room's furnishings."

"Exactly," Trout agreed. "The killer didn't take it for that reason. It looks like a fixture of the room. If the highboy wasn't so tall, you would have noticed it before now."

Ginger shook her head. "I think we should call Duncan."

"Fine." Trout took his cell phone from his back pocket and took a couple of photos of the box. "Call him. These shots will show it as we found it but I'm not waiting for him to open it."

"Trout..."

"Don't worry, Ginger. I won't touch anything. I just want to see what's inside." He took a tissue from the holder and slipped the ivory toggle from the embroidered slot. He glanced at Ginger then lifted the lid.

Inside the box was a clear plastic bag filled with what looked like gray sand.

Ginger released a sigh of relief and reached out to touch it. Trout caught her hand.

"I wouldn't if I were you."

"But it's nothing. Just some kind of dirt or..."

"If it's what I think it is, we'd best leave it for the police."

"What do you think it is?"

"Someone's cremated remains."

"Oh my God." Ginger turned into Trout's chest and his arms came around her. "Oh my God."

He held her for a long minute in a light embrace, allowing her the time to absorb the nature of their discovery. Finally, she pulled free of his arms and turned her face from him.

"Sorry. I'm just feeling a little overwhelmed, I guess."

"No problem. It wasn't what I was expecting either." He watched her compose herself and thought how easy it would be to get accustomed to holding her. She turned back to face him.

"We'd better call Duncan," she said.

"I should have listened to you." He jangled the change in his pocket. "I'm sorry."

"Waiting to learn what was in it from Duncan wouldn't have changed anything." She glanced around the room. "I don't know if I'll ever be able to get past two bodies in this suite. It'll never be the same."

"Try to look at the bright side."

"There's a bright side?"

"You can now qualify for the Ghosts and Gravestones tour."

"Not helping, Trout."

"Just trying to lighten the mood."

"The only thing that's going to lighten the mood is to find out what's going on at the Paradise."

"Agreed."

"So, how do we do that?"

"Maybe Duncan's made contact with Liberty's boss or a family member. I think we need to find out why she was in Key West. Maybe we can then figure out if her death is related to what she was doing here or if it has some other root cause."

Ginger took a tissue from the holder and gently lowered the lid of the box back in place. She didn't fasten the clasp. "My phone's in my room. I'll call Duncan. For now, I guess we should leave things as they are and lock the door."

"I think I'll stand guard on the landing." Trout regretted his words as soon as they were out of his mouth. The cloud of worry seemed to deepen in Ginger's expression. "He'll want to know we had eyes on the situation until he gets here."

She merely nodded and headed down the stairs.

Trouble sat on a hall table, his green gaze fixed on Trout.

"You should be happy now," Trout said to him.

Trouble leapt lightly to the floor and trotted down the stairs after Ginger.

"Fine," Trout said.

DUNCAN WASN'T BEST PLEASED when Ginger told him that she and Trout had opened the box. He arrived at the Paradise in less than fifteen minutes of her call, a lab tech following on his heels.

"What the hell, Ginger?"

"Sorry, Duncan. We wanted to be sure it had any significance."

"Right." Her explanation did nothing to erase the glower on his face. "Do me a favor and let me be the judge of what has significance in the future."

"Sure." She watched him bound up the stairs followed by the CSI tech. After a moment of indecision, she climbed after him. She wasn't going to be left in the dark.

When she and Trout tried to enter the room after him, Duncan turned to them and barked, "Out."

Two uniformed policemen arrived along with another

detective and an additional CSI tech. One of the policemen shooed Trouble away from the door of the Toucan Suite then asked Ginger and Trout to wait downstairs in the sitting room. The look on Duncan's face when she started to protest their exclusion made her think twice. Reluctantly she and Trout descended to the lobby and waited.

The Talents returned from an excursion at the height of all the hubbub. Ginger held her breath that they would demand to be checked out but instead they displayed mild curiosity and because they weren't allowed to go up to their room, decided to spend the wait time by the pool in the shade of the palm trees.

Harry, Ginger's part-time bartender, didn't come on duty until five when Ginger knew they were housing so few guests. Normally she could keep an eye on people lounging by the pool while she worked in the kitchen. She sent Angela to man the tiki bar with instructions to give the Talents whatever they wanted in an effort to defuse any further blowback. She then programed the bed and breakfast's land line to transfer to her cell.

In short order, Annette Benoit came down the stairs in a huff, her late afternoon nap having been interrupted by the police demanding access to her room. Ginger didn't think free booze would soothe those ruffled feathers as Annette sailed through the Paradise to the courtyard.

When Duncan finally came downstairs Ginger and Trout waylaid him. "Well?" she asked.

"Most likely burned remains. Probably human from the amount of ash."

"How can you tell?" Ginger asked.

"I've been a cop a long time. And that's what the CSI

believes it to be at this point. He's thinking it's from a crema-
tion, which would be the good news," Duncan said.

"And the bad news?" Ginger felt her heart thumping in
her chest.

"It could be the barbeque variety."

Trout swore under his breath. "Jesus, could you be any
more callous?"

Duncan looked at Ginger and what could have been a
shadow of regret swept briefly over his features. "Sorry. It's
probably the former. We should be able to determine which in
the lab."

"How?" Ginger asked.

"The evenness of the burn, if there's any other debris in the
ash. That kind of thing."

"Great," Trout said.

"Yeah, well, just remember the techie is pretty sure it's the
former. That makes my job easier. All we have to do is find out
who in Ms. Anderson's life has died recently."

"Have you been able to contact her family?" Ginger asked.

"Not yet. Talked to the boss. He was hot under the collar
about how she spent her time while here. Apparently, the USDA
monitors their employees' social media. She worked for their
enforcement branch. The purpose of her visit was supposed to be
to determine if the Hemingway cats were in violation of the
federal court order. Or, rather, that the management at the
museum wasn't doing its job. Apparently, there'd been a complaint
that the staff was being lax in following the AWA guidelines."

"Wait," Trout said. "What are you talking about? What
does the Department of Agriculture have to do with cats?"

"The museum was sued some years back under the Animal
Welfare Act because someone didn't think the cats were being

properly cared for. That's under the jurisdiction of the USDA."
Duncan shrugged. "They fought in the courts for years but a
decision was finally handed down in 2013, I think. The
museum lost. So now they're monitored by the federal
government."

"I can't believe what you're saying." Trout glanced at
Ginger for confirmation. She nodded. "Were the museum cats
being mistreated?"

"Of course not. They're the most pampered animals in the
contiguous forty-eight states but you know how the government is. The urge to have a finger in every pie is like catnip to
any regulating agency. And once they had a citizen's complaint
it was all over but the shouting." Duncan took his pinging cell
phone from his jacket pocket and read a message. "If you want
to know my opinion, I think the Hemingway cats serve as an
excuse for federal employees like Ms. Anderson to have a nice
vacation in Key West on the government's dime."

"That would explain all the photos of the cats she took. I
couldn't get my head around that because she didn't like cats,"
Ginger said.

"Perfect for the job, then." Duncan slipped his phone back
into his pocket. "Look, I've got to head over to the station.
Don't worry, Ginger, I'll let you know what we find out about
the ashes. We've taken the rest of Ms. Anderson's belongings
and printed every inch of the room and landing. Sorry about
the mess but it's all yours now."

"I can clean it?"

"Yep. You might want to get one of the girls to do that.
You're supposed to take it easy for a few days."

"Don't worry," Trout said, "I've got it covered."

Duncan gave him a long assessing look. "Uh huh." With
that he strode across the foyer and out of the Paradise.

CHAPTER FIVE

*S*o, Megs and Bartholomew aren't as barmy as I thought. Under the circumstances, I can understand their paranoia to a degree. Though they do take themselves far too seriously, in my opinion. It's not like their lives are in danger or that there's a federal prison for wayward cats. Still, it could be that they would lose their freedom and that's something to be guarded against. A cat is a natural hunter and the call of the wild still stirs our blood. Fortunately, my people have the good sense to recognize that fact.

Could sanctions from the government be motive enough to kill? I don't think so. This is Key West in August, after all. It's much too hot and humid to expend the energy necessary to commit murder. Unless there's a lot better reason than wandering cats.

But it also brings to mind the young man we encountered on the return from Trout's boat yesterday. His whole aura was a cornucopia of all things cat, including litter. Liberty did photograph him with Megs in his arms. Could he be another of their spies?

That brings us back to square one. The mystery still remains as to why Liberty had a box full of someone's ashes in her room, and who

that someone might be. Maybe that's at the heart of it all. Until we
identify the remains we'll never know.
    Right, then. It's time I nudged Ginger into action.

TROUBLE SLIPPED between Ginger's legs as she and Trout
watched Duncan pull out of the parking bay of the Paradise.

"What do you think?" Trout asked. "Will he keep us in
the loop?"

"Fifty-fifty, I'd say. He's pretty unhappy about the box of
ashes. And the cell phone."

"That's the impression I got."

"It's an ego thing, too, I imagine. Duncan does like to be in
charge." She realized how that sounded as soon as it was out of
her mouth. Thankfully, Trout let it slide.

"So, what do you propose we do?" he asked.

Ginger turned toward the rear of the building. "I saved all
Liberty's photos and call log to my phone. Duncan hasn't had
any luck contacting her family so I suggest we try."

"You sly dog," Trout said with a grin. "Who knew you could
be so devious."

"It wasn't deviousness. I need to save my business, if that's
still possible. This whole dead body, box of unidentified ashes,
and guests rousted from their afternoon nap isn't going to do a
whole lot for my bottom line." Ginger hoped that the very real
fear she was experiencing didn't show in her voice. She didn't
want to come across as one of those helpless women who fell
apart when things got tough. The Paradise wasn't only her
business, it was her home and her history. She had to save it.

"I'm surprised by the Talents," Trout said. "You'd think
with all this mayhem a young couple celebrating their first

anniversary would be falling all over themselves to get away from such macabre happenings."

"I think the operative words are *first anniversary*." Ginger grinned. "As for Mademoiselle Benoit, she's expecting some kind of business connection and hovers near the phone day and night. And she's French."

"I don't know what being French has to do with anything but she didn't sit home waiting for the phone to ring last night."

Ginger opened the door to her quarters and sat at her desk. "How do you know?"

"She was still out when you got knocked on the head and she didn't return until shortly after two this afternoon. I got the impression she wasn't out at a business meeting."

"How could you tell?"

"Well," Trout smiled, "she stayed out all night and when she came waltzing in she had that certain look about her. As you said, she's French."

Ginger laughed. "Men."

"'Tis true I'm but a mere man but I've had years of training in observation. I report to you only what I saw and my deductions from it."

"Very noble of you." Ginger booted up her laptop and took out her cell phone. "Let's start with the numbers she called in the time before she got here. The police have probably checked likely listings in her contacts and the obvious ones like her boss. They may not have gotten around to someone she calls less frequently. Hopefully that someone will answer the phone for an unfamiliar caller from Key West."

"You do that and I'll look through these photos and see how many local spots I can identify."

Trouble hopped onto Ginger's lap and placed his forepaws on the edge of her desk. "Yeow."

Ginger scratched his ears and said, "Not now."

Trout scrolled through the shots on the phone's camera while Ginger used the landline to dial a number listed under Babs.

"Here's a picture of Jerry." Trout said. "I'm sure he'll remember her. Marilyn is his favorite pin-up."

Ginger clicked the speaker button on the desktop phone.

"Hello?" A female voice answered.

Trouble's ears twitched and Ginger sat forward in her chair. "Hi," she said. "I'm trying to reach a family member of Liberty Anderson."

There was a pause on the other end of the line. "Who's this?"

"My name is Ginger Browne. I own the Paradise Bed and Breakfast in Key West."

"Why are you looking for Liberty?"

"Are you related to Ms. Anderson?"

"No." Another pause. "She's a friend. You said the Paradise? Isn't that where she's staying?"

"Ms. Anderson is a registered guest here. The police have been trying to reach her family. There's been an accident."

"Oh, dear. Is she in the hospital? Is it serious?"

"Can you tell me why Ms. Anderson came to Key West?"

There was another brief silence. "This is something serious, isn't it? Is Liberty all right?"

"It would be better to get the details from the police. Do you mind telling me your name?" Ginger held her breath hoping the woman wouldn't hang up on her.

"Barbara Delinsky. Liberty and I used to work together. I quit to be a stay at home mom."

"And she came to Key West because of work?"

"The Hemingway cats. It's a plum assignment. There's a regular rotation of the field agents so everyone gets a trip eventually. Normally it's just a couple of days of fun and sun for routine checks but when there's an actual complaint, whoever is up for the next assignment is guaranteed at least a week in paradise."

"Did she say she was meeting anyone here?"

"No. But I haven't talked to her in at least a couple of months. I only know what's going on from her Facebook page."

Trout was mouthing the word family and Ginger nodded.

"Is there a family member I could call, a husband, mother, or father?"

"No." Another pause. "Her husband left her six months ago. It's been a really bitter legal battle. His name is Arthur. I don't know how to get in touch with him but I don't imagine he'd be concerned about her accident. They weren't married that long. Less than two years, I think."

"And there's no one else?"

"Not that I'm aware of. She had a lot of friends but I never thought they were close, you know? More like party friends you see out all the time but not the kind you stay in and watch a movie with or go shopping."

Trout was jotting notes on a pad during the conversation. He wrote BOYFRIEND? in block letters and showed it to Ginger.

"Was she dating, do you know?"

"I couldn't say. All I know of the past few months is what she's posted on Facebook and tweeted. I knew she was on the roster for the next site visit. She kept posting photos of Key West, recipes for margaritas, night life pictures in anticipation of her turn. When the complaint came in it was naturally assigned to her. She posted about it as soon as she heard. That was about two weeks ago. She was thrilled. But she hasn't mentioned anyone in particular in her life. Though it might not be something she'd want to plaster all over Facebook right now with the divorce and all." Another pause. "Have you called her boss?"

"I understand the police have talked to him."

"He'll probably be able to tell you who to contact. There should be someone listed in her employment file in case of an emergency."

"Thanks." Ginger looked at Trout and gestured with her hand for any other questions he might have. He shook his head. "I appreciate you speaking with me."

"Is...is Liberty dead?"

"The Key West police department can answer your questions Mrs. Delinsky. Ask for Detective Moore."

"Oh my God."

"Thank you, Mrs. Delinsky." Ginger hung up the phone. Her hand was shaking. She looked up at Trout. "I didn't know what to say. I should have realized she would ask."

"You did the right thing." He took her hand in his. "There's no easy way to tell someone about a death. You did great."

"Then why do I feel like a dirty, rotten scoundrel for calling that poor woman out of the blue and scaring her like that?"

"She would find out eventually. This way, maybe we can get a jump on a motive. A bad divorce is a good place to start." He turned the laptop around so he could access the keyboard. "Let's see if we can find Arthur Anderson. He's probably living in DC or Virginia. We'll start there."

Trout typed the name in the search bar. After a couple of

seconds, he said, "Wow. Who knew there could be that many Arthur Andersons."

"Duncan has probably already gotten his name and contact information from her boss."

"Yes, but Duncan isn't sharing." Trout typed some more and the people finder page showed a less daunting list of names but still more than it would be feasible to contact. "I wonder what Arthur's middle name is."

"Try legal filings. If they're getting a divorce there should be court records."

"Good idea." Trout typed and clicked across several links then sat back from the computer. "Whoa."

"What?" Ginger looked up from the screen of her phone.

"This doesn't look good." He turned the computer so she could see the display.

"Oh my God."

TROUT COULDN'T BELIEVE his eyes. There on the computer screen was a photograph of a man he remembered seeing on Liberty's phone. The problem was, the photo on the computer accompanied an obituary notice. Arthur Langford Anderson died eighteen days ago. Cause of death unspecified. He was survived by his ex-wife, Melissa Harper Anderson, and his current wife, Liberty Nielsen Anderson. The guy looked to be ninety if he was a day.

"That explains the box of ashes." Trout glanced up at Ginger.

"I bet she was going to spread his ashes in the ocean." Ginger leaned back in her chair. "That's why she chartered your boat."

"Could be. Who writes an obituary listing the ex-wife?"

"The ex-wife."

"Right," Trout said. "Wonder what the cause of death was."

"He was ninety-one."

"That would do it. We need to tell Duncan. "

Ginger picked up the phone and dialed then tapped the speaker button. When Duncan answered she said, "Hey, Trout and I found some information on the ashes."

"Arthur Anderson," Duncan said.

"Right, well, we thought you'd want to know."

"The Key West Police Department isn't totally incompetent, Ginger. We can occasionally find our rear ends if we're allowed to use both hands."

"I wasn't trying to do your job, Duncan. I just want to know what's going on at the Paradise before I lose everything."

There was a brief pause before Duncan said, "You should leave it to me, Ginger. I'll get to the bottom of this. Now that we're pretty certain the ashes belong to Ms. Anderson's deceased husband, we're back to the rohypnol overdose scenario. My guys are canvassing all the local hot spots. It's just a matter of time and manpower."

"Great. Thanks."

"I know that tone of voice." Duncan's sigh came through the speaker. "For once don't be so pig-headed."

"Right." She hung up.

Trout had enough sense to keep his mouth shut. Into the silence Jules called from the nether regions of the bed and breakfast proclaiming he was on the premises and ready for duty.

After a few moments Ginger said. "How's that list coming? Did you identify any of Liberty's watering holes?"

"A few. I've experienced a great many of Key West's bars but not all of them."

"Let's start with what you've got. I can't sit on my hands and wait. If the killer came back for the phone, I want to know. If not, then what did he want?"

"Let's go see if we can find out." Trout saw the fire of determination in Ginger's eyes and knew she wouldn't stop until she had some answers. He wasn't about to let her go on the hunt for a killer on her own. There were a number of iffy places around Key West as there are in any city, not the least of which was the Oriole. It wasn't that far from the marina and he'd been known to frequent it from time to time. It wasn't the kind of place for a woman to be on her own, especially if she was asking difficult questions.

At last, we're actually going to do something. Surely there will be plenty of people who remember Liberty. Though she was no friend to me, it appears she could be quite charming to humans, particularly male humans if her photo gallery is anything to go by.

I spy Megs through the window of Ginger's room. Bartholomew can't be far. The two are inseparable although I think it's purely a platonic relationship considering how uninhibited she is around me. The ladies do love my sleek black coat and I've been told more than once that I have bedroom eyes but it's the accent that makes them sigh.

Ah, well, no one can compare to my Veronica so it's back to work for me. Megs and Bartholomew can keep tabs on the Paradise while I accompany Ginger and Trout. They will need my fine deducing skills, not to mention my keen sense of smell if we encounter our murderer.

The plan is to work through the places captured on Liberty's phone. It would perhaps be more time efficient if we started at the last place she photographed but Trout seems to think it would be better to get the full picture and learn how her night progressed. I can't argue with his logic.

There's nothing to distinguish the Green Parrot from any number of other bars in Key West save a variety of wooden parrots and strings of green lights delineating the seams of what looks like an upside-down multicolored umbrella over the bar. In reality it's some kind of parachute material. A sign proclaims the date 1890 as, I assume, the founding of this establishment. I'll take their word for it. The walls are covered with slogans, paintings, and photographs. The bar itself appears to be well stocked with both alcohol of all sorts and people, also of all sorts. I recognize the pool table as one of the photo props Liberty used.

Trout engages the bartender, a man with no hair on his head but a ferocious mustache. This is the aforementioned Jerry who is enamored of Marilyn, whoever she may be.

"I remember her, all right," he says with a heavy Aussie accent. "She'd be hard to miss, hugging up on all the guys at the bar and generally pissing off all the women."

"Any guy in particular that took a fancy to her?" Trout asked.

"I already told the cops. No one was shunning her, but I don't think anyone did more than enjoy the attention."

"Did she leave with anyone?"

"No. She sat at a table with a fat mate in a white linen suit and they had their heads together for a bit but he was still sitting there when she left."

"Did you know the guy?"

Jerry shrugged. "He's been in here a few nights, mainly just crowd watching and drinking dark beer. He does like his pint. Another blond joined him at the table last night and they had their heads together for a good little bit but he didn't leave with her either. I know that for sure."

"Oh?"

Jerry grinned but said nothing.

"You don't know who he is?" Trout asked.

"*Well, he certainly wasn't a conch or a regular either.*"

"*Would you recognize him if you saw him again, you think?*"

"*Sure.*"

A patron on the other side of the bar began clamoring for a drink. As Jerry turned to see to his other customers, he leaned back over the bar and said, "Sorry about the dead body, Ginger."

"*Thanks, I guess.*"

"*Don't worry, everyone is spreading the word that the Paradise is the best bed and breakfast in town.*"

Ginger laughed. "Don't oversell it, Jerry. I can't afford any more disappointed guests."

He gave her a brief salute and turned to his customer.

There's nothing to see and no one to question at the zero mile marker for U. S. Highway One so we move on to the next photo op.

Margaritaville is a madhouse of people trying to talk over each other and the music as they drink and wait to be seated for dinner in the outdoor restaurant. No one working here remembers seeing Liberty either outdoors or inside but it's now two days since she passed this way and for most of the wait staff one tourist looks pretty much like another. I sympathize with their plight.

We have no better luck at Sloppy Joe's and now that we've reached the Chart Room Bar all of us are ready to take a breather and regroup. I confess this is my preferred choice for a little nosh. There are those who would turn their noses up at a hotdog but then they haven't had a hotdog at the Chart Room Bar. If it's good enough for the Rockefellers and Jimmy Buffett, then it's good enough for me. Quite delicious, actually.

It's not crowded here and the bartender has time on his hands to answer our questions. He tells us he has only just come on duty after being off the previous evening. He confesses that he was about to cut Liberty off when her friends decided to help her back to her hotel that night.

"*Did you tell the police this?*" Ginger asks.

"*Like I said, I got off at three that morning and haven't been back at work until now.*"

"*What did her friends look like?*" Trout wants to know.

"*A young couple. I didn't realize they knew her at first. They came in after her and sat at a table. It was only when she began insisting on another drink that they came over and helped her to her feet.*"

"*How do you know they were her friends?*" Ginger asks.

"*They called her by name and she seemed to recognize them.*"

Well, now, here's a clue indeed. Was this some acquaintance she acquired since arriving in Key West, I wonder. Or did someone follow her here from Washington, DC?

Trout takes some cash from his pocket and pays for their drinks. "*What time was this?*" he asks the bartender.

"*Must have been about one. Something like that. Regulars start to arrive about then, so, yeah, about one.*"

The bartender takes the money and rings up their drinks.

"*Do you think it was the Talents?*" Trout asks Ginger.

"*No. It was about one when Trouble started acting up outside the Toucan Suite. I looked to see if Liberty's key was on the hook. I was afraid he was going to wake her. The Talents' key was gone so I knew they were already in for the night.*"

"*We need to identify this couple. This is the first we've heard of her knowing anyone here in Key West.*"

"*That's not exactly true,*" Ginger said. "*After I left your boat yesterday I ran into a man on the steps of the Paradise. He was looking for Liberty.*"

"*Who was he?*"

"*I don't know.*"

"*Did you tell him she was dead?*"

Ginger shook her head. "*I didn't know what to tell him so I fudged a little. He wouldn't leave his name or a message. Just said he'd catch her later."*

"Could that have been our would-be rapist?"

"At the time I didn't know about the rophynol so it didn't occur to me to be suspicious. The truth is I thought he looked kind of nerdy."

"What did he look like?"

"Cary Grant with glasses. Except a very slim version of Cary Grant. And he had a lot of curly hair."

"So not really Cary Grant."

"He had the dimple and the voice."

"The voice?"

"Well, he didn't say Judy, Judy, Judy, but he had that cultured drawl."

"Not a native then."

"No, but I got the impression he met Liberty after she arrived in Key West."

"How so?"

"He said they had just recently met. She'd been in town three days. I don't know, that's just what I thought at the time."

Trout sat in thought for a minute. "Maybe someone she worked with? Did anyone think to ask if this was Liberty's first assignment to check on the Hemingway cats?"

"I don't know."

"Do you have your phone?"

"Yes."

"Let's see if the bartender can identify these friends from the photos you copied from Liberty's phone."

I'm beginning to think Trout has potential. Perhaps his former profession has made him more intuitive than most bipeds. And now that he's in the picture as to a person of interest, maybe we'll get somewhere.

· · ·

TROUT WATCHED the bartender scroll through the photos. He shook his head. "Can't help you, man. I don't see them in any of these shots."

"Thanks." Trout handed the phone back to Ginger. "Did it strike you as odd that the couple didn't acknowledge Liberty when they first entered the bar?"

"It's possible they didn't see her when they first came in and only became aware of her when she got loud and demanding."

"It's a small bar."

"True." Ginger looked around the room. "Too small, in fact."

"According to what we know, she wasn't exactly hiding her candle under a bush. So, the question becomes, why didn't they acknowledge her when they came in."

"Good question. Maybe because she was drunk and they didn't want to get roped into her evening. They could have decided to step in when it looked like she was going to get into trouble. Maybe they realized from her behavior that something was wrong."

Trout shelled a peanut and ate it, his focus on the wall behind the bar, his mind chasing something on the edge of his memory. It wouldn't come so he let it go. "What next?"

"Do you think she went to the Oriole? There aren't any pictures from there that I can tell. So much of what she took after she left here is out of focus and could be any number of bars. Maybe she'd forgotten all about the Oriole but it almost seems as if she was working her way in that direction. She did ask you about it earlier in the evening."

"I can't see her friends taking her there if she was as drunk as the bartender said."

"Then where did she go? She wasn't at the Paradise."

Trout shook his head. "You hungry?"

"You just ate a hotdog."

"It's way too early to get answers at the Oriole so we might as well get something decent to eat. A hotdog just doesn't cut it for me."

"What then?"

"My place. We're almost there and Sawyer has some snapper from my last catch in his freezer." Trout wasn't sure why the invitation popped out of his mouth. In truth, it was too early to find anyone at the Oriole that would likely have encountered Liberty. The late-night crowd would be the best bet in that endeavor. He supposed the invitation sprang from his need to keep an eye on Ginger, to prevent her wandering into trouble on her own in pursuit of a killer. *Yeah, right*, he thought.

At that moment Ginger's cell phone rang. She looked at the caller ID. "It's the Paradise." She touched the green button on the phone and held it to her ear. "Paradise..." She frowned. "Wait..." She listened. "What do you mean, she wants the ashes?"

Trout had been watching the cat who had invited himself along on their little jaunt across Key West. Ginger's comment got his full attention and that of the cat. When Trout raised his eyebrows in a questioning look, Ginger shook her head and shrugged.

"Okay, okay. I'm on my way back. Ten minutes. Just tell her to wait."

Ginger ended the call. "You'll never guess who's at the Paradise."

"So tell me."

"Mel Anderson, as in Melissa Harper Anderson, first ex-wife of Arthur Anderson, who, by the way, is also known as Arty."

"The plot thickens."

"Indeed it does. She's demanding Jules give her Arty's ashes."

MEL ANDERSON WAS AN OLDER, less endowed version of Liberty. Two vertical lines were permanently etched on her forehead. Her tomato red lips pulled down in a frown. She turned on Ginger the moment she walked through the door of the Paradise.

"Tell this idiot to give me Arty's ashes. I'm the executor of his estate and I have every right to them." She waved a rather battered sheath of papers before Ginger's face.

"And you are?" Ginger asked.

"I've already told this moron. I'm Arty's wife. I'm here to retrieve his ashes. That slut stole them from the mausoleum." Mel's face grew a deeper red as her voice pitched higher. "I'm suing them, too. They should have had security on the premises. But no, not Forest Springs. They don't even have cameras." Her gestures were becoming more out of control as her agitation grew.

Trout stepped forward and said, "You're upset, Mrs. Anderson, and rightfully so. We want to help you resolve the problem. Would you like a cup of tea?"

"Got any gin?" she asked but Trout's words and tone were already having an effect on her.

With a glance Ginger sent Jules scurrying in the direction of the tiki bar. "Let's move into the sitting room and get comfortable. Jules will bring you something to calm you down."

"As long as it's gin," Mel said.

"I'm sure it will be," Ginger replied. "This way." She made a sweeping gesture with her hand and Mel Anderson preceded them from the foyer. Ginger gave Trout a small smile of thanks then the two of them trailed behind Mel into the sitting room.

Jules arrived with the gin, placed it on a coaster on the small table beside Mel's chair and quickly escaped to just beyond the entrance to the room, his ear cocked to, no doubt, capture the conversation that was about to ensue.

Mel took a bracing gulp of gin then stared at first Ginger, then Trout. "Well," she finally said into the silence. "Where are Arty's ashes?"

"The police have them." Ginger said.

"Police? Why would they have them? Don't tell me those idiots in DC had them confiscated. They could hardly be bothered to take the report."

"Why do you think Liberty stole them?" Trout asked.

"To deny Arty his last wish."

"What was his last wish," Ginger asked.

"To have his ashes at Forest Springs next to me. We planned everything, matching urns and all. That piranha was only ever after his money. But she didn't get that either." A malicious smile spread over Mel's face and her eyes positively sparkled with delight.

"Who did get it?" Ginger asked.

The smile disappeared. "That hasn't been settled yet. She claims he made a new will but he didn't." Tears formed in Mel's eyes. "I know Arty didn't do that to me."

"How did you know where to find Liberty?" Trout's question was softly spoken.

"Facebook, of course. The witch has been posting pictures for four days. She's having a ball, drinking and partying all across Key West." A tear escaped and trailed down Mel's cheek. "Poor Arty. He was such a fool. He's barely dead and she's sleeping with every man who crosses her path."

"How long were you and Arty married?" Trout asked.

"Fifteen years." Mel sniffed. "We were happy."

Ginger thought they couldn't have been that happy if Arty divorced her and married Liberty. As to Arty wanting to spend eternity entombed next to Mel, that was also doubtful. The fifteen year length of their marriage also suggested that Arty had married Mel when she was about Liberty's age. She wondered if the latest divorce proceedings had been fueled by yet another Mel/Liberty lookalike. "When did you get here, Mrs. Anderson? Where are you staying?"

"I just got here. Flew into Jacksonville then took a puddle jumper here. Had a four hour layover. Could have driven it in that amount of time." She took another drink of her gin. "I booked a room at the Pier House before I left Virginia but I came straight here. I didn't want to risk Liberty skipping town before I got Arty's ashes."

Ginger tried to think like Duncan. How much should she reveal to the grieving ex-widow? "How long are you planning to stay in Key West," she asked.

"Just tonight. It's too expensive down here and that's coming from someone who lives in spitting distance of the capitol. I thought winter was the height of the season for Key West."

"We really don't have much of an off-season anymore. August isn't our busiest month, for sure, but prices don't fluctuate as much as they once did." Ginger glanced into the foyer, looking for Mel's luggage. "Did you send your bags on to the Pier House?"

"No." Mel lifted a purse the size of a diaper bag. "Since I'm only here to get Arty's ashes, I'm traveling light. Didn't want the bother and fuss of being strip searched at the airport." She drained her glass of the last of the gin. "I'm going to wait right here until that hussy shows up and I'm giving her a piece of my mind."

Ginger shared a look with Trout. "I'm afraid that's not possible."

"You kicking me out?" Mel's expression was turning aggressive again.

"No," Trout interposed. "Liberty isn't coming back to the Paradise."

"Checked out already?"

"No. The police have her."

A smile spread across Mel's face. "Hot damn! Don't tell me they arrested her. For stealing Arty?"

Obviously, the thought that Liberty might have been arrested gave Mel great pleasure. It also reinforced what Ginger had already decided. Mel Anderson didn't know what had happened to Liberty.

"She's at the morgue, Mrs. Anderson. She's dead."

CHAPTER SIX

*D*etective Moore sent a patrol car to pick up a very gleeful Mel Anderson. If her story hadn't been so believable, I would consider her our number one suspect. One is unlikely to pronounce their undying hatred of a murder victim unless they know they're in the clear. The good news is that the ashes have been dealt with and we can get on to the matter at hand. Unless there's another ex-Mrs. Anderson lurking out there somewhere, we still have no idea why Liberty was murdered.

Ginger and Trout are in the kitchen together cooking up some heavenly smelling dish of shrimp in a sauce over wild rice. A bottle of wine is breathing on the work table. The conversation has moved away from dead bodies, ex-wives, and poison.

I feel very much a third wheel. Were I not so famished I would give them their privacy. But at last dinner is served. Not only is Ginger a fine pastry chef, she's a whiz at quick, easy, gourmet dishes that would thrill the soul of Gordon Ramsey. Though I can never forgive him the disastrous renovation of the Coffee Pot in New Orleans, I confess he is the measuring stick by which I judge all chefs.

I am replete, having eaten every last morsel of shrimp. Now I shall *take myself off before the kitchen gets any hotter. I've never seen two adults dance around their attraction for each other so much.*

There's no sign of Megs or Bartholomew. I daresay they... What is that I smell? I do believe it's our killer! Where is it coming from?

I put my nose to the air and am off. He has the gall to return to the scene of the crime a third time. Yes, he stood here in the shadow of this mahogany tree spying on the Paradise.

Let's see where his scent takes us. If only I could risk the time it would take to alert Ginger and Trout but I dare not lose his trail. Never mind. I will find and identify him. Justice for Liberty is only a matter of time now.

GINGER FELT FLUSHED from the heat of the kitchen. That's what she told herself anyway. An evening that started out as a search for a killer had turned into an intimate dinner in the kitchen of the Paradise. She was feeling the wine but she was also feeling the attraction of a handsome man, one she had been drawn to for months. No more wine she told herself then he opened the fridge and took out another bottle.

"Why don't we take this out by the pool, what do you say?"

"That would be nice. It's too hot in here."

Trout worked the corkscrew then caught up their two glasses and headed for the back door.

Ginger took off her apron, ran her fingers through her hair, and told herself to keep things platonic. She had enough problems at the moment and didn't need to add the uncertainty and demands that a relationship would throw into the mix.

For a late August night, it was surprisingly cool. At least it was cooler than the kitchen. The up-lights in the palm trees and the glimmer of the pool lights made a lovely setting for a couple ending a busy day in paradise.

It occurred to Ginger how rarely she took advantage of her home and its amenities. It felt good to lie back in an outdoor lounge chair and sip the oaky chardonnay. She resolved in that moment to do this more often.

Trout sighed and took a sip of his wine. "This is the life."

A response about the long hours and hard work was on the tip of Ginger's tongue but she stopped herself in time. She wanted to enjoy the moment, to be simply a guest in her own establishment enjoying a glass of wine and the company of a handsome man. "Yes," she said. "It is."

"How long have you run the bed and breakfast?"

"Always. Well, my grandmother ran it then my mother. I've lived and worked here my whole life. I inherited it four years ago."

"You're a native, then."

"A true conch of the Republic."

"Why do the locals call themselves conchs? I know generally it has to do with the sea snail, that it's a popular dish down here but how did that turn into an identity for the locals?"

"It's part of the local lore. After the American Revolution the people loyal to Britain fled to the islands but then the British government began to tax their food just as they had the colonies. They declared they'd rather eat conch than pay taxes. In protest they came up with dozens of ways to prepare it. Over time, the natives became known as conchs. It's not exactly the Brahmins of Boston but it designates the old families who settled here. Sawyer is descended from one of those old families. Nowadays you don't have to be a blue blood, you just have to have been born here to be considered a conch."

"That's nice. Belonging is important."

Ginger heard a hint of longing in his voice. She let the silence settle around them. All was quiet except for the distant voices of people on the street and a faint thread of music drifting on the night air. It was a comfortable, intimate bubble of companionship. After a time she asked, "Do you miss your old life?"

Trout didn't answer immediately. Finally, he said, "It's hard to know what I feel. Sometimes I have guilt about bailing when I know there are so many kids who need help." The quiet returned and they sat amiably sipping their wine.

Trout cleared his throat. "I couldn't do it anymore. Not after Missy's death. I worked with her for over a year. She'd be placed in a home then after a few weeks she'd disappear to the streets again." After a long pause he said, "'She left a note. *I told you I wanted to die, Dr. Richardson.* That's what she wrote."

"Oh, Trout. I'm sorry."

"Yeah, well, me too. But not for myself, for that scared little girl who had nowhere to turn. No one to protect her. She simply couldn't live with her demons any longer." He cleared his throat. "She was only fourteen." He drank down the last of his wine, leaned his head against the cushion of the lounge chair, and closed his eyes.

Ginger felt the sting of tears and knew she couldn't trust herself to speak. Her throat was tight with grief for a troubled young girl and for the man who tormented himself with the knowledge he couldn't save her.

THE EVENING HAD BEEN GOING SO WELL, Trout thought. Over the course of the meal Ginger had let go of her worry about the fate of the Paradise. It was just as well that she brought up his former life. Trout had let down his guard. Her nearness did that to him. He couldn't afford to let Ginger into his life. Her or anyone. It was just too painful to care.

He wanted to pour another glass of wine but wouldn't let himself do it. For all that he didn't want to get any closer to Ginger, he didn't want her to see him in a bad way. He lay there on the lounger with his eyes closed trying to decide how long he should stay. She would feel bad about bringing up the topic if he left immediately. He didn't want to ever do anything to make her feel bad. As Duncan had said, she was good people.

A rustling sounded in the staghorn ferns. Trout opened his eyes to see a really fat cat waddle from the low foliage surrounding one of the palm trees. It was soon followed by a much smaller cat. They stopped and stared at him and Ginger, then carried on across the patio, onto the back porch, and up the stairs leading up the outside of the building to the second floor.

"Where'd they come from?" he asked, glad for something to distract from their earlier conversation.

"Hemingway cats. That's Lou Costello and Mitzi Gaynor."

"With crossed eyes?"

"I guess they didn't realize her eyes would be that way when they named her. And I don't know of any Hollywood actress with crossed eyes so whoever she was named after was going to be an imperfect fit."

"Why not give her a different name, then?"

"Tradition. All the Hemingway cats are named for Hollywood stars."

"I should probably do the tour."

"It's interesting," Ginger said. "It brings a lot of tourists, that and Mel Fisher's museum."

They were making small talk, trying to get past the awkwardness of his earlier confession, Trout realized. He was forming the words of an excuse to leave in his mind when a woman's scream pierced the night.

Trout and Ginger jumped to their feet and looked toward the bed and breakfast. The front door of the Paradise slammed against the outer wall from the force of a slim figure dressed in black flying down the front steps. Trout took off after the fleeing man.

THE SCENT HAS BROUGHT *me to Mallory Square. The culprit is up ahead somewhere. Ah, what's this? A fat man sitting on an iron bench looking out over the water. He's the source of the scent. He reeks of it. How can this be? Whoever knocked Ginger unconscious was slender and agile. She remembers him fleeing quickly down the stairs. The man before me could hardly walk down a flight of stairs much less run down them.*

I have no choice but to use the oldest of the tried and true methods of a gumshoe, a stakeout. This man is involved in the happenings at the Paradise. Could he be the man Liberty talked with at the Green Parrot? He certainly fits Jerry's description, right down to the white linen suit.

He's checking his watch. Our suspect is waiting for someone. I shall wait with him. He is oblivious of my presence. This will be a piece of cake. I'll just move closer so I can hear his conversation when his accomplice arrives.

"Hello, cat," the fat man says. "Haven't I seen you somewhere before?"

I ignore him. It's a good thing cats are known for being rude and indifferent. Surely he can't suspect that I'm a super sleuth hot on his trail.

"I've seen you, or a cat very like you. Are you the Paradise cat?"

I move beyond him and under a nearby tree. A flock of chickens squawk and flap their wings. I've disturbed them in their roosting place. Whatever possessed the good citizens of Key West to allow chickens to roam the streets at will? Cock fighting is a cruel sport but does it necessarily follow that the good citizens must allow them to now roam freely as retribution for past sins? I slink away under the shadow of the tree and they begin to settle. I make my way back to the fat man on the bench but this time I am behind him.

From his movements I can tell he's checking his watch again. He sighs heavily. "Where are they," he mumbles.

Time crawls by. The pedestrian traffic along Mallory Square has died away to an occasional tourist. The fat man sighs again and starts the process of shifting his immense weight from the bench. Just as he has managed some momentum, a couple comes hurrying toward him. I recognize them immediately.

"Well?" the fat man says.

"Nothing," Mr. Talent says.

"Nothing?"

"She must have it somewhere else." Mrs. Talent's voice holds a note of apology.

"Hmmm." The fat man heaves himself to his feet. "This bears some thought. Where could she keep it if not in her room? Does the Paradise have a safe?"

"Yes, but there's nothing in it." Mr. Talent looks down and sees me. "Isn't that the black cat from the Paradise?"

The fat man turns and sees me. "Yes, I believe it is. He followed me here earlier."

My cover is blown but I see no reason for concern. They can't possibly know I'm on to them.

"Forget the cat, Ray," Mrs. Talent says. "What are we going to do?"

"I have something in mind," the fat man says. "I'll have to think through the details. Wait until you hear from me." With that he turns and heads back along the square at an ambling pace.

I'm torn as to who to follow and decide it's best to know as much as possible about the fat man. The Talents will be at the Paradise. I *can find out what they're up to later. For now, I'm tailing the fat man.*

What could he be after? It certainly isn't Arty's ashes. Ginger and Trout thoroughly searched the Toucan Suite as did the Key West police department. Twice. There wasn't a hint of what could be at stake. Whatever it is, at least I now know that it would fit into the safe of the Paradise.

We continue along Wall Street, the fat man in no particular hurry. I assume that's because his weight prevents him from having a second gear. I confess that surveillance isn't my favorite activity but then he stops and I am encouraged.

He stares into the window of a shop. The sign proclaims it to be Cigar City USA. The fat man searches the inner pocket of his white linen jacket, then tries the door. It's locked at this late hour. The fat man sighs and moves along. I foresee a long night ahead of me.

WHOEVER RAN from the screaming Annette Benoit and the Paradise was fast and knew the lay of the land much better than Trout. Within two blocks he had lost his prey. Checking dark driveways and dense foliage only got him barking dogs. When he got back to the bed and breakfast Ginger was replenishing Annette's snifter with brandy.

Ginger looked up as he came through the door. "Anything?"

He shook his head. "What happened, Ms. Benoit?"

"Someone was in my room." She pushed a heavy wave of blond hair back from her forehead. Her face was pale but she wasn't the weepy, hysterical type. "I opened the door and he shoved right past me." She took a drink of the brandy. "I screamed."

"Did you get a look at him?"

"No." She gestured with her hand, a downward motion from her forehead to her chin. "He wore, how do you say in English, ...over the face."

"A ski mask."

"No, no. It was...how you say...funny...like, um, clown." She looked from Trout to Ginger and back again. "How did he get in my room? The key was on the hook when I came back to the hotel." She took another sip of brandy then said, "How did he get in?" It was less a question this time and more a matter of puzzlement.

Trout and Ginger exchanged a look. How indeed did someone get into the Bird Cage without the key. Ginger went behind the desk, opened the top drawer and held up the ring of master keys.

"Can you think of any reason someone would want to break into your room? Did you leave jewelry, money there? Your passport?" Trout asked.

"No. I do not bring fine jewelry when I travel. And my money and passport are with me." She gestured toward her purse on the seat of the sofa.

"There was nothing else of value anyone would want?"

A spark of something flashed across Annette's features but was so quickly gone that Trout couldn't be sure he had seen it. She averted her eyes, shook her head, and fiddled with the glass of brandy, turning it round and round in her hands.

"How did he get in?" She glanced up at Ginger. "If I hadn't broken the heel of my shoe he would have come and gone and no one would have known."

"I don't know," Ginger said, "but I intend to find out. Jules was supposed to be on the desk tonight. There's no sign of him." She took out her cell phone and dialed his number. A muffled voice saying 'It's the boss, pick up the phone. It's the boss, pick up the phone,' could be heard.

Ginger lowered the phone and turned in the direction of the voice. "That's Jules' ring tone." She took off toward the kitchen. The pantry door stood partially open. Coffee grounds were scattered all over the floor of the pantry and out into the kitchen. The soles of Jules' high tops were clearly visible. Ginger stepped over his sprawled legs and knelt beside his inert body. "Oh my God."

Trout was on her heels. He felt the artery in Jules' neck. "He has a pulse." Then he gently moved Jules' head enough to see the deep bloody gash on his forehead. "Call Duncan and an ambulance."

He helped Ginger back across Jules' legs and took out his phone. After he snapped several photos of the pantry and Jules' from different angles, he opened a kitchen drawer and found a clean cloth. He held it to Jules' wound and the young man moaned.

"I GOTTA TELL YOU GINGER, you're keeping me up nights, and not in a good way." Duncan said as he surveyed the kitchen and pantry floor. "Why would he be in here?"

"He was probably doing the set-up for breakfast."

"Umm. That's the routine?"

"Yes."

"The intruder must have come in the back door. Otherwise there would be no need to bash the kid's brains out."

"Really, Duncan." Ginger crossed her arms and looked away to hide the fear she felt.

"Sorry," the detective said. "He'll be okay. He couldn't have been out long if the French dame screamed and you and Romeo came running."

Ginger ignored Duncan's little dig at Trout. "It was at least fifteen minutes, maybe twenty."

"How so?"

"Well, he would have to knock Jules out, take the key and go upstairs, unlock the door to the Bird Cage..."

"Where'd you get all those crazy names for the rooms?"

"My grandmother." Ginger gave him a look that said don't go there. "Anyway, he'd have to bring the key back down..."

"Why?"

"Because Ms. Benoit said the key was on the hook when she came back to the Paradise because of her broken heel."

"Doesn't make sense."

"Will you let me finish?"

"Sure, sure." Duncan shrugged and slapped his notebook against his thigh.

"He'd have to return the key, go back upstairs to the room and be there when Ms. Benoit came in and surprised him. He pushed past her, she screamed, Trout took off after the intruder and I came through the kitchen to the foyer and found her at the top of the stairs."

"You didn't see the kid in the pantry when you came in the back door?"

"No. It's off to the side as you can see, and the back entrance lines up with the door into the dining room. I ran straight through. It never occurred to me to look."

"So, the boat captain takes off..."

"His name is Trout."

"He takes off after the intruder, you go to the aid of your guest. Then what?"

"Ten or fifteen minutes later Trout's back. He lost the guy. We were trying to determine from Ms. Benoit if she had anything that would be the target of a burglar. The problem, as you observed, with how the man got into her room made me remember that Jules should have been on the desk. I called his phone and that's how we found him, by following the ring tone."

Duncan stared off into space for several seconds. Finally, he sighed, slapped the notebook against his thigh again, and said, "First a woman dies from alcohol and GHB. She's in a locked room. Everything locked up tight. No way for anyone to have been in there with her. Now we have a woman return to her room to find a thief rummaging through her things in a room that's locked, the key on the key board. How's that possible?"

"You're the detective."

He nodded. "Right. Tell me again why you didn't see whoever it was coming in the back door?"

"We were out by the pool. Our backs were to the main building." Ginger felt the blush creeping up her throat.

Duncan stared at a spot somewhere above Ginger's head, a thoughtful expression on his face, and nodded again. "Right." He turned toward the door into the hallway, stopped, and looked back at her. "Where is he now?"

"He went to the hospital with Jules. He said he'd stay with him until his mother got there."

"I'll talk to the Benoit woman. Looks like you could use a cup of coffee. Or tea."

"I'm fine."

"Quit worrying so much."

She nodded. Easier said than done, she thought. It was almost as if someone had it in for her and her business. She frowned. No, that couldn't be it. Sawyer Daniels wanted to buy the Paradise but that didn't have anything to do with what was happening. He knew she would never sell and it was more a joke between them than any real intent on his part. There was no one who would benefit if the Paradise closed its doors.

Ginger gave herself a good mental shake and went about the business of tidying up the coffee from the floor of the pantry and the kitchen. The police had dusted the door and anything the intruder might have touched. She took a bucket of warm soapy water and began scrubbing away the mess they left. There would still need to be breakfast for Annette Benoit and the Talents.

Duncan stuck his head around the door of the kitchen when she was cutting fruit for the next morning. "I've done all I can. Too many guests, too many prints for what we've collected to be of much value, but we'll run them and see if we get any hits. Give me a call if you need me."

"Sure. Thanks, Duncan."

He nodded and turned to leave.

"Duncan," Ginger said, "it was the same man. There was a scent in the air of the landing. It was there last night, too. When he pushed me into the stair railing."

Duncan came into the kitchen, a frown creasing his forehead. "Why didn't you mention this before?"

"I didn't realize it until tonight. When I ran upstairs to check on Annette the odor was lingering in the air and I knew it was the same man. I think it was in Liberty's room as well when I found her. I can't be sure but I remember a scent I couldn't place when I first opened her door."

"What is it you smelled?"

"Tobacco. More specifically, cigars. You know, that slightly sweet aroma of a good cigar."

"So, our would-be burglar slash murderer is an aficionado of fine cigars, is that what you're saying?"

"I don't know what else would explain the scent being present each time we have a break-in."

"Right," Duncan said. "It's not much to go on but you never know when some little something like that will trip up a bandito." He gave her a searching look. "Are you going to be okay here on your own until your friend returns?"

She nodded. "Thanks. I think all the blue lights and commotion would scare away even the most determined villain, don't you?"

He nodded. "If you're sure. I could stay you know."

The offer made Ginger hesitate for a split second but not because she felt she needed protection. It was because she needed someone but it wasn't Duncan. She shook her head. "Thanks, but I'm fine."

"Okay." He watched her a moment longer, then nodded. "Okay," he said again and went out the door.

Ginger finished the breakfast preparations, locked the back door, and turned out the kitchen lights. She fluffed pillows on furniture, picked up the empty brandy snifter, and generally tidied the foyer and sitting room. At the reception desk, she glanced at the key board and straightened the note pad, pens, and credit card machine. Her hand stilled as she dropped the ring of master keys into the drawer. She looked back at the key board. The Talents' key wasn't on its hook.

Surely they hadn't been so involved in each other that they had been unaware of the break-in and the police all over the place. Again.

"Yeow!" Trouble called from the front porch. His forepaws appeared and disappeared several times just above the wood that formed the bottom panel of the beveled glass door as he scratched at it to get her attention. Ginger sighed. "Crazy cat." She unlocked it and let him in. "Where the devil have you been? You need to quit wandering the streets before you get lost. I don't have time for your foolishness."

The cat ignored her and shot up the stairs to the second landing. At the top he turned and looked down at her. "Yeow!"

Ginger followed after him and saw that for once he wasn't obsessing about the Toucan Suite. He went straight to the Talents' room.

CHAPTER SEVEN

*G*inger is reluctant to follow me upstairs. I have to make her see that the Talents aren't what they appear to be. I blame myself, of course. Shoddy work on my part, I confess. Benedict Cumberbatch would never allow a perceived explanation to stand. He would have looked at the evidence before his eyes. I must bring the bipeds into the picture.

Finally, she's beginning to realize that something is amiss. She knocks on the door of the Macaw Suite. There's no answer. She knocks again and calls out, "Mr. Talent, Mrs. Talent? Are you in there?"

Silence.

She looks down at me.

"Yeow."

"Right." She rushes downstairs and returns with the master keys. Once again, she knocks and says, "Ray, I'm coming in."

The bed is made, and the towels stacked in the bathroom are neat and tidy. A lipstick and some foundation are on the dressing table as is a notepad with some figures on it. One of the Paradise's lush bath robes is draped across the easy chair, another one on the foot of the bed. Otherwise, the room looks little used.

Across the room, one of the floor-to-ceiling windows onto the gallery is open and the room is quite warm. If a murder on the premises doesn't kill business, then the power bill will. Poor Ginger, the cards are definitely not falling in her favor.

I investigate the room, checking the armoire, highboy, and the bathroom. At the threshold of the window I discover the strong scent of both Talents. They have traversed this way many times. What is it out here that is such an attraction?

The lounge chairs on this end of the gallery appear to be little used. A layer of pollen covers the seat of one of the chairs and the table top. Ray Talent's scent is present as is that of his wife, but it's faint. It's the path to and from the other end of this lovely covered outdoor space that holds their scent more strongly. The Talents seem to have been intensely interested in the Toucan Suite.

Ginger follows my lead and stands before one of the windows into the Toucan Suite. Tentatively she places a finger under the check rail and pushes. The bottom panel of the double hung window glides upward with a familiar squeak.

The sound of a car door closing draws us to the railing of the gallery. We see a taxi pulling away from the bed and breakfast and Trout coming up the front walk.

TROUT LOOKED up at the sound of Ginger calling his name.

"Up here," she said.

She was waiting on the upstairs landing when he topped the stairs. The door to the Toucan Suite stood open as did the door to the room on the other end of the front facing hallway.

"I've got something interesting to show you." She led the way to the end room. "This is the Macaw Suite," she said. "The Talents' room."

She walked through the door, over to the windows, and out

onto the gallery. She looked back to see that he was following her. "The window was open like this when I came up here a few minutes ago."

With that, she crossed the gallery to the windows opening from the Toucan Suite. The window stood open. "It wasn't locked when I tried it just now but the door to this room was."

"You think the Talents have been using the gallery to get into Liberty's room?"

"The cat thinks so."

Trout looked down at Trouble who sat on his haunches on the gallery floor and watched him with his steady green gaze. "The cat showed you this?"

Ginger hesitated. "Well, sort of." She blushed. "I had just realized that the Talents hadn't made an appearance all through the investigation of the attack on Annette. I mean, no one could have slept through all that commotion, you know? And I assume the police knocked on their door to see if they heard or saw anything. I don't know for sure, but either way, they weren't here."

"Maybe they didn't want to get drawn into another incident. How can you know with certainty that they weren't here?"

"The key. It wasn't on the board. That's how I know whether all my guests are in or not. They aren't supposed to leave the premises with the key."

"Maybe they forgot. It could have been unintentional."

"It's big and heavy with a large emblem on the ring. You would notice that much bulk and weight in your pocket."

"But maybe not so much a woman's purse." Trout suggested.

Ginger didn't seem convinced. "Maybe. But what about the window to the Toucan Suite? It was locked when we tried it."

"I remember."

"That was after I came home from the hospital. They had hours. The Talents could have been fast and loose with the room keys. At almost any time, really, even before Liberty died. They could have looked for whatever it is that started this whole thing in motion since the day she checked in."

"Wouldn't that be a big risk? What if Liberty came back to her room when they were in there?"

Ginger considered that for a moment. "There are two of them. One could be tailing her while the other searched the room."

"I suppose."

They stared at the open window as if it would give them the answer.

"It would be tricky." Trout said. "Either you or Jules could have caught them out."

"True. Or Angela. But this is a lean operation. All of us wear a multitude of hats. Anyone paying attention would see that they had plenty of opportunity."

"And they'd have access to all the room keys."

Trout saw the look of dismay his comment caused. "It's not your fault, Ginger. We don't even know they had anything to do with her death. Or that they were ever in this room. Duncan's team was in here just hours ago. They could have left the window unlocked."

"Oh, my stars," Ginger said, "I didn't even ask about Jules."

"He's fine. I left him with his mother clucking around him as he posted photos of his bandaged head on SnapChat."

That made Ginger smile. Trout thought she had a beautiful smile. It engaged her whole face, especially her eyes.

"Jules will milk this for all he's worth," she said.

"We'll get him a case of orange Jello."

"Orange?"

"That seems to be his favorite."

Ginger's smile faded. "Oh, Trout, what am I going to do? This has to stop. What if this maniac had killed Jules?"

Trout took her in his arms in a loose embrace. She relaxed against his chest. "We'll find whoever's behind this," he said.

"And if we don't? If the Paradise ends up on the Ghosts and Gravestones tour, the B & B where people go to die?" She leaned her head back to look him in the eye.

"Well," he said, "I guess I'll have to hire you to crew on the *Baby Buddha*."

She laughed and buried her face in his chest.

"It does lend itself to some catchy promotions. I'm sure Jules could come with any number of slogans. *On your way to paradise? Check out at the Paradise.*"

He felt as well as heard Ginger's muffled laughter against his chest. They stood that way for a couple of minutes. Trout knew the moment she became self-conscious. He released her from the embrace as she pulled away.

"What now?" she asked.

"You should call it a night. I'll man the desk. I'm curious to see what the Talents have to say for themselves."

"I can't ask you to spend another sleepless night on my behalf." The brief respite from worry was fading from her features.

"What are friends for, right?"

"But..."

"No buts. Jules isn't the only one with a lump on the head."

"Trout..."

"I wouldn't sleep anyway. Curiosity killed the cat, you know." He shot Trouble a glance and could have sworn the cat gave him a look of disdain.

. . .

GINGER GAVE in to Trout's insistence that she leave him in charge. She couldn't convince him that all his effort would be wasted because she was too wired to sleep. Maybe it was because she was so wired that she gave in. Usually, she was calm and in control. This internal turmoil was new to her. Now, in her bed in her pajamas, she tossed and turned.

After twenty minutes, she gave up and went to her desk to make a list. It was one of the tricks she had learned from her grandmother. When the demands of the day wouldn't let go, write them down, then rewrite the list by priority. Doing so freed the mind of fear that something important would be forgotten. This wasn't exactly a list of things that needed to be done but hopefully, the process would have the same affect.

She decided to write down everything that happened from the time Liberty Anderson checked into the Paradise. First, she noted the guests in the Flamenco Suite were already on the premises, having checked in two days earlier. Another couple had one of the cottages near the pool.

Liberty arrived late Monday afternoon. The room overlooking the pool and the gardens didn't suit her. She wanted one of the more spacious rooms on the front of the bed and breakfast. Since she was willing to pay the higher rate, Ginger switched her to the empty Toucan Suite. As soon as Liberty checked in and deposited her bags in her room, she had gone out.

The Talents, Ray and Crissy, arrived at about nine on Tuesday morning. Ginger sat back in her chair and tapped the notebook with her pen. Why hadn't she realized this before? Now she saw their arrival so soon after Liberty checked in as suspicious.

She gave herself a mental shake. No jumping to conclusions, she told herself. At this point it was all circumstantial. State the facts, she told herself, and see where they lead.

I'm glad Trout insisted on manning the front desk tonight. I suspect Ginger could hold her own in most circumstances but we're dealing with a murderer. The Talents have some explaining to do about their involvement in whatever it is that's going on at the Paradise. The problem is, will Trout know which questions to ask?

My night thus far hasn't been a total waste. I was able to gather some information by tailing the fat man. First off, his name is Fortesque. Secondly, he's staying at the Curry Mansion Inn. That means he has boodle to spare. He likes pear brandy for a late-night cordial. And the staff all have a frightened look on their faces when he sits in one of the wicker settees on the verandah.

None of this tells me anything about the object he's pursuing but at least I know where to find him should the need arise.

Well, it's been a busy night. I confess to being rather foot sore. I might as well settle in for a nap until the wayward guests in the Macaw Suite decide to return. Trout is, at the moment, alert and on the job. A smart cat always naps when the opportunity presents itself.

TROUT YAWNED AND STRETCHED. He had weathered the night by burying his nose in *The Guards*, a novel by Ken Bruen. The writing was good and it kept him turning the pages. He hadn't trusted himself to take advantage of the day bed in the small cubby behind the reception desk. Two nights without sleep made the desire to drowse too strong. So, he had ousted the cat from the comfy chair in the foyer and stretched his long

legs before him and read until the sun came up. The Talents
hadn't returned to the Paradise.

He wandered into the kitchen. The coffee pot was set to go
so he flipped the switch and watched until it finished gurgling
and hissing. With a cup in hand, he strolled through the downstairs of the bed and breakfast. All was quiet. Even the cat had
abandoned him.

When he had finished his coffee, Ginger came through
from the kitchen with a small coffee carafe and a plate loaded
with fruit and fresh pastries. "Thanks for starting the coffee,"
she said. "Hungry?" she asked as she refilled his cup.

"Starved."

She placed the plate on a table for two in the bay window
of the dining room and went back through to the kitchen.
When she returned she had another plate, napkins, and silverware. "There's orange juice if you like."

"Thanks. This is great." He sat down in the chair that gave
him a view of the side and front lawn of the Paradise and
slathered a scone with butter. "No luck last night. The Talents
didn't return to the nest."

"You think they're not coming back?"

"Can't say. All they left in the room was a little make-up,
toothbrushes, and a few articles of clothing, not even a
complete change for either of them. Not a big loss for most
people." He took a drink of his coffee. "I can't see how they fit
into the equation. But if they are involved, why wouldn't they
return unless they've found what they were searching for?"

"Maybe they know we're on to them," Ginger said.

"That's just it. Are we on to them? Are they involved?"

"I think they are." Ginger took the list she made the night
before from her back pocket. "I couldn't sleep so I made a
timeline of events since Liberty registered. Ray and Crissy

Talent arrived in the early morning after she checked in the previous afternoon. There were no flights arriving at the airport until eleven."

"Maybe they came by car."

"No. Taxi." Ginger ate the mango on her plate.

"Okay. We should check the address they gave when they registered. And their credit card."

"I already did. The address is for a drugstore in Nashville. They paid cash for their room. Five nights in advance. They're good for one more night."

"No credit card?" Trout asked.

"Yes, there's a credit card. The world can't function without a credit card in this day and age. I scanned it against damages or bar charges."

"But?"

"I can't access their financial information. The police would have to do something like that."

"They might still show up. It could be they partied all night in a bar and will come dragging in later." Trout drained his coffee cup.

"Do you think that?" Ginger asked.

"Not really. The false address clinches it. The only problem is we don't know why they were surveilling Liberty."

"Back to square one."

Trout nodded and then dug into the food on his plate. He was hungry, tired, and not feeling particularly sharp this morning.

"I'm going to be off in a few minutes," Ginger said. "They're releasing Jules from the hospital and neither he nor his mother has a car. I need to do some shopping for incoming guests on Wednesday as well." She hesitated. "I hate to ask, but could you man the fort until I get back? It won't take long.

Angela will be here soon but I can't leave her alone under the circumstances."

"Sure. I planned to hang around a while anyway, just to see if the Talents did show up."

"Thanks. I'll be as quick as I can."

Angela had arrived at some point while they ate. She came through from the kitchen and poured him another cup of coffee. Ginger shook her head to a second cup and took her plate to the kitchen.

Trout sipped coffee and looked down Ginger's timetable. Monday, Liberty Anderson arrived. Tuesday, Ray and Crissy Talent checked in about nine in the morning, Wednesday afternoon, Annette Benoit had a late arrival due to flight delays. Liberty died some time Thursday night. Ginger surprised the intruder on Friday night. Annette found the intruder in her room on Saturday night. He put the sheet of paper on the table, closed his eyes, and let his mind float.

The sound of someone clearing his throat woke Trout from a light snooze. He looked up to see a man of medium height and weight standing beside his table. He looked to be Hispanic, possibly Cuban, Trout thought. He straightened in his chair. "Can I help you?"

"I'm sorry to disturb you," the man said, "but there seems to be no one about. I'm looking for Ms. Benoit. Would you know her?"

"She's a guest here. Is she expecting you?"

"Yes and no. We were to meet for a business transaction but we seem to have gotten our wires crossed. I thought I'd just pop around and speak with her."

"You're local?"

"Yes."

When no other information was offered, Trout stood and said, "I don't know if Ms. Benoit is in her room."

"Can you tell me which room she's in?"

"How about I call and see if she's in and if she wants to come down to meet with you?"

"You work here?"

"Not officially. Just helping out this morning." Trout went into the foyer and to the reception desk. He glanced at the key board, picked up the phone, and rang the Bird Cage. After a number of rings with no answer, he frowned and returned the phone to the receiver. "She must have gone out already."

"I see," the man said. He studied Trout for a moment then said. "Perhaps I'll have better luck later."

"Can I give her a message, say who came calling?"

"That's not necessary." The man smiled, crossed the foyer, and went out the door.

"Huh," Trout said.

As GINGER STORED the shopping items in the refrigerator and pantry, Trouble came sauntering in through the back door, asking to be fed.

"Why should I?" she asked him. "If you'd been here earlier you'd have gotten a hot breakfast."

Trouble just looked at her and blinked.

"Right," she said. "Let's see if I remembered cat food."

Trouble flicked his ears forward and turned his head to the side in a look of long suffering.

Ginger laughed. "You're funny, you know that? Let's see what I have."

She broke up a scone and added a dollop of strawberry jam then a dollop of clotted cream. "That should do you," she said as she placed the concoction in his bowl on the small mat designated as Trouble's food station. "*Bon appetit.*"

Trouble gave the dish a sniff then began to eat.

"Where have you been, I wonder," Ginger said as she opened a recipe file and began flipping through the worn and stained cards. "The Paradise is suddenly over run with cats. Lou Costello and Mitzi Gaynor are hanging around here a lot more than usual. I think they want you to come out and play."

Trouble gave a violent flick of his tail and looked up at Ginger, ears flattened.

"You really should stay closer to the bed and breakfast. Something could happen to you. Then where would I be, huh? Tammy Lynn is one of my oldest and dearest friends and she's very attached to you. She said you were smart as a whip, so be smart and stop wandering off."

"Who're you talking to," Trout asked as he came into the kitchen.

Ginger felt her face grow hot. "Myself. Trying to decide on something different for afternoon tea. I like to provide enough finger food so my guests can skip either lunch or dinner if they want. It's so expensive to eat out all the time." She laid the card aside, and leaned against the work table, supporting her upper body with her forearms. "I get tired of making the same old things and though they're new to my guests, well, I guess I'm unsettled right now. Looking for something to keep me busy."

"When did you get back?"

"A few minutes ago. I've been putting away the food. And feeding the cat."

"How's Jules?"

"He says he feels fine. Not even a headache but I doubt that. He wants to come back to work but the doctor said he should take it easy for at least three days. He needed twelve stitches."

"Ouch."

"Yeah, tell me about it."

"What did the intruder hit him with?"

Ginger nodded toward a rack of open shelves. "One of the tall pepper mills. It was the sharp corner of the base that did the damage. They found it in the pantry where the attacker threw it under the shelves used for all the table linens."

"Will he be able to return in time to help with the convention crowd?"

"I can't let him even though he needs the pay check. As you know, everything in Key West is expensive. He helps support his mom. This will be a hardship on them. She works as a maid at the Curry Mansion Inn."

"Yeow! Yeow!"

"What the devil..." Trout looked over at the cat presiding over an empty food bowl.

"Who knows," Ginger said. "He's probably still hungry. I suspect he's been out tom catting all night."

"Isn't he, you know, fixed?" Trout asked.

Ginger's voice dropped to a whisper. "Yes. Still, the streets are full of cats and, well, who knows. What nature intended and all that."

She glanced up at Trout and saw he was watching her, a wicked grin on his face. She felt the heat crawling up her throat. Why in the world had she said that? "Any news from Duncan, about the prints?" She said as she picked up the recipe card and studied it.

"If he had any news he wouldn't be calling me."

She heard the humor in his voice and sighed. They were both well past the blushing teenage years. She looked him in the eye, shook her head, and smiled in return. "Grow up already."

"I feel all grown up at the moment."

"You're just sleep deprived."

"Is that what it is?"

Ginger found she couldn't hold his gaze so she turned and picked up Trouble's empty bowl and took it to the kitchen sink. He began to twine between her legs and kept talking as if he needed to impart something to her.

"Are you still hungry?" She asked.

Trouble sat, looked down at the floor, then at her, and finally at Trout. With that he headed to the back door. He sat there, facing the door, his back to them as if giving them the brush off.

"Fine." Ginger crossed the kitchen and opened the door. "Stay close," she said to his disappearing back. She returned to the work table. "If something happens to him I'm dead."

"Don't worry, he's a smart cat. Besides, he has nine lives and he's black."

"What does being black have to do with it?"

"Lucky. Black cats are lucky, didn't I tell you? Especially on and around the water."

"If that's true, why don't I feel lucky?"

Trout had no answer for that.

"Well," she said, "I guess I need to clean the Macaw Suite. Even if the Talents are coming back." She looked up at Trout. "No sign of them while I was gone, huh?"

"No," he said, "but something curious happened."

"What?"

"A man came looking for Annette."

"What's so curious about that?"

"I'm not sure exactly." Trout walked over to the windows

overlooking the back patio and pool. "Something about it seemed off, you know?"

"Off how?"

Trout glanced from the view to Ginger with a sheepish expression on his face. "I fell asleep in my chair. I was still in the dining room. Don't know how long I was out but it couldn't have been more than a few minutes. And I woke up to find him standing over me."

"You've had a long couple of nights."

"He said he had a business meeting with Ms. Benoit but that they kept missing each other."

"She's been obsessed about messages. When she goes out for any reason that's her first concern when she returns. Did anyone call."

"It wasn't that, exactly. He wanted to know which room she was in."

"You didn't tell him, did you?"

"No. Especially after the intruder in her room last night. If he didn't know already then he wasn't going to find out from me. And to be truthful, the fact that he asked didn't bother me at first. It seemed like the kind of question anyone would ask, you know. Like, hi, I'm looking for Dr. Doolittle, do you know his room number? It was only when he wouldn't leave a message or his name that I decided it was odd."

"Like someone trying to see if she was really a guest here?"

"I guess. I mean, how difficult can it be these days to connect with a business client? Everyone has cell phones, text messaging, voice mail. Why couldn't he connect without coming to the Paradise on the off chance he would catch up with her?"

"I agree. What did he look like?"

"He wasn't your slim, geeky Cary Grant. He was Hispanic.

No accent though so I'm guessing he's a US citizen or has lived here since he was a kid. My thought at the time was that he could be Cuban. Well dressed, linen slacks, nice shirt. He smelled of cigars."

Ginger inhaled sharply. "That was the scent when I opened Liberty's door. It was a cigar, slightly sweet but very distinctive." She moved to Trout's side. "It's the same man who knocked me out and broke into Annette's room."

"We don't know that. Besides, how could he have gotten out of Liberty's room? The door was locked from the inside."

"Through the Macaw Suite. He could have gone out the window, along the gallery to the Talents' room, down the stairs and out the front door with no one the wiser. It was late, no one on the desk. It could have happened that way." Ginger nodded a self-satisfied nod, "They're in it together."

"It makes a certain kind of sense. There's only one problem. What do they want that they thought would be in Liberty's room?" Trout ran his hand through his hair and tugged at it as if that would stimulate his brain and give him an answer. "Besides that, he asked for Annette. Why the interest in Liberty's room if he's looking for Annette?"

"There's a connection between the two women," Ginger said. "We need to find out what it is."

"Whatever it is," Trout said, "it got Liberty killed."

"Do you really think so?"

"Yes, I do."

"What about the date rape thing?"

"A cover for the real goal."

"What's that?"

"I have no idea, but I'll bet Annette does."

CHAPTER EIGHT

*G*o out to play with the other cats? Really? Is that what Ginger thinks of me, that I'm no more than a kitten, looking for a ball of twine or...or... Really! A cat's entitled to some modicum of respect. I see no hope for her. After all the bother I went to in showing her the culpability of the Talents she still thinks of me as a brainless nitwit.

Speaking of which, here are Megs and Bartholomew in the shade of the tiki bar. My hope that they could be useful in this investigation has long since been dashed. Between the two of them they couldn't manage a straight answer if their lives depended on it. Inbreeding aside, I had expected more. They are, after all, cats.

"Still looking for the killer?" Bartholomew asks then yawns hugely. He looks as if he will topple over at any moment into a dead sleep.

"Been up all night?" I ask in reply.

"As have you."

"How would you know that?" I ask.

"Oh, we get around, don't we Megs?"

Megs stops trying to follow the flight of a butterfly and looks at me.

At least, I think she's looking at me. "Busy night," she says. "Busy, busy night."

"Doing what?" I inquire.

"Watching," she replies.

"Anyone or thing in particular?"

"The other spy."

Crickey. These two are impossible.

Bartholomew falls over and begins to snore.

"There were other cats here recently. Have you seen them?" I ask.

Megs' eyes open wide. "Other cats? What are they doing here?"

"Not much apparently. I was curious if they were also Hemingway cats."

"I don't know."

"Maybe if I told you their names you might."

"Oh. Well, maybe."

"Lou Costello and Mitzi Gaynor."

Bartholomew snorts in his sleep.

"That's me and Bartholomew," Megs says. "Our daily names."

I stare at her, not certain she understood what I told her. "Daily names?"

"Yes. The names people call us. Not our particular names."

"You have more than one name?"

"Three, actually. Don't you?"

Bartholomew coughs and wheezes as he opens his eyes and rights himself. "Are you totally illiterate?"

I'm stunned by his accusation. I'm a cat of superior intelligence, a cat with the power of deduction far greater than that of men. Yet when I'm in the presence of Megs and Bartholomew I feel as if I've fallen down the rabbit hole.

"Why do you have three names?"

"Why don't you?" Bartholomew coughs again. "Do you at least have a singular name?"

"A singular... I suppose I do. My name is Trouble."

Bartholomew and Megs exchange a look then he lies back down. "Where did you say Wetumpka was?"

"In Alabama."

"Strange customs they have in Alabama." He yawns and closes his eyes.

Definitely the rabbit hole. "Okay, Megs, what's your third name?"

"Oh, you never tell your singular name. Never, never, never."

"Why not?"

"It's written that the singular name is one you never confess, it's the name that you know yourself to be, a name no one can ever guess."

"Who wrote such a nonsensical thing?"

"It's a classic, my good man," says Bartholomew without bothering to open his eyes. "You should come by the museum and enlighten yourself with some worthwhile literature. Start with T. S. Eliot and go from there. I have grave doubts about Wetumpka."

I can't believe I'm wasting my time on this nonsense. It's time to get back to the business at hand.

"Look," I say, "the murderer has been lurking around the Paradise. I caught his scent last night and followed him. While I was on his trail, someone broke into the bed and breakfast and burgled one of the rooms.

Megs nods. "Yes. The other spy."

"The burglar is also a spy?"

Megs blinks at me as if I have two heads. "No, silly, he burgled the room of the other spy."

"Annette Benoit is a spy?"

"Yes," Megs says, her voice dropping to a conspiratorial whisper.

I had a busy night last night and not much sleep. Talking with Megs and Bartholomew doesn't help. In fact, it leaves me with a sense of confusion, a state I definitely don't enjoy. I must find a cozy spot and rest if I'm to be at the top of my game. I think I'll try the swing on the front porch of the Paradise. There's always a lovely breeze there.

. . .

GINGER HUNG UP THE PHONE. "Duncan says he'll put out a BOLO for the Talents. The information they gave him is the same we have."

"They're long gone by now." Trout said.

"Maybe. If they got what they were after you're probably right."

The door of the Paradise opened and Sawyer Daniels walked into the foyer. "Hey, Ginger. Trout. What's up?"

"Helping Ginger out. She's shorthanded right now."

"Yeah. Heard about the dead woman, Ginger. I guess the law sorted it all out?"

"They're working on it," she said.

"Got any coffee?" Sawyer hitched his shorts up a notch on his belly.

"Sure. Come into the kitchen." She glanced at Trout. "How about you? Want another cup?"

"No thanks," he said but trailed along behind Ginger and Sawyer. "What brings you to the Paradise, Sawyer?"

"Annette Benoit."

"Oh?" Trout and Ginger said in unison.

Sawyer laughed. "Yes. We have a business meeting in about fifteen minutes."

"What sort of business?" Ginger asked.

Some of the humor left Sawyer's face but he shrugged good naturedly and said. "She has something to sell that I want to buy. At least she thinks I want to buy it."

Sawyer lived in a small apartment down near the marina and he dressed like a down and out bum, complete with several days growth of whiskers. But Ginger and most of the conchs on Key West knew he was in fact a very wealthy man. He bought things on a whim like the classic sailboat he had Trout refinishing. The money earned by the marina probably didn't cover the costs of maintaining it. Sawyer's money was old family money, the kind that seemed to grow without any effort on Sawyer's part. She was dying to ask him what Annette could possibly have to sell that would interest him but checked herself.

She poured coffee and cut him a slice of banana nut bread. "Here you go. Sorry to sound so nosy but weird things have been going on around here and I was surprised when you said you had business with Annette. She's French."

Sawyer gave a belly laugh. "What's that got to do with anything?"

Ginger smiled. "I know, I know. It's just that she's foreign, I guess."

"She's supposed to be in possession of a lost treasure. Very mysterious about it," Sawyer said.

"Like Mel Fisher's Atocha treasure?" Trout asked.

"I don't know. She said she knew I was a collector and that she had something that was thought to be lost forever, something she knew would be of interest to me."

"So you agreed to meet with her just like that?"

"Why not? She came to me. All I had to do was walk a few blocks for the sales pitch." He took a bite of the banana nut bread.

"That's funny," Trout said. "You're the second guy looking for Annette this morning. He said he had an appointment with her too."

"She must be trying for a bidding war." Sawyer said. "Who was the other guy, if you don't mind telling me."

"I don't know. Hispanic, maybe Cuban. He wouldn't leave his name."

"Ummm," Sawyer said as he ate another bite of the bread, "you're a fine cook, Ginger."

Ginger wanted to ask more questions but controlled the impulse. Annette had been waiting for a phone call for days. It would appear the expected call was from either Sawyer or the nameless Hispanic. Mystery solved. Sort of.

"You want me to ring her room and let her know you're here?" Ginger asked.

"I don't think she's in," Trout said. "I called her room for the other guy and she didn't answer even though her key isn't on the board."

"She could have been in the shower," Ginger said but the sudden change in Trout's expression and the pounding of her heart said it could be another reason entirely.

TROUT AND GINGER raced from the kitchen and stared at the key board behind the registration desk. Annette's key wasn't there.

"How stupid could I be," Ginger wailed. "I should have secured the keys after what happened to Liberty. What was I thinking?"

"Don't jump to conclusions. Get the master key. Let's see if she's in her room."

Ginger grabbed the ring of master keys from the reception desk drawer. They hurried up the stairs. She took a deep breath and knocked on the door of the Bird Cage. No answer. She knocked again and said, "Ms. Benoit, it's Ginger Browne. I'm coming in."

She placed the key in the lock then looked up at Trout. "It's unlocked."

The door swung open on silent hinges. The room was

empty. Someone had slept in the bed at some point after it had been made-up the previous morning. A dress lay across the easy chair and a pair of high heeled sandals looked as if they'd been kicked off and left where they fell. Two of the towels had been used.

"Where's the fire?" Sawyer said from the open doorway.

Ginger jumped when he spoke and pressed a hand to her chest. "Uh, it looks... it looks like she's gone out."

Sawyer looked at his watch. "Maybe she's on her way back. There's still a couple of minutes before we were supposed to meet."

"Right." Ginger swept her hair back from her forehead. Her hand was trembling. "Right. We should lock up the room and go back downstairs."

When she passed through the door, Sawyer said, "What's going on, Ginger? You look pale as a ghost."

"It's a long story."

"I like long stories."

"It's not for the local gossip mill."

"My lips are sealed."

She studied him a moment. "Come downstairs. I need a drink."

"Now you're talking," he said.

Trout took the keys from Ginger and locked the door of the Bird Cage. "When did you make your appointment with Ms. Benoit?"

"Yesterday afternoon. She called and said she was having a little difficulty meeting up with a local authority on the treasure. That was the reason I hadn't heard from her. It wasn't anything to be worried about, she assured me, because she had already been to Boston and spoken with an authenticator there."

"Where in Boston?"

"She didn't say. It was all hush-hush. I debated even meeting with her because, to tell the truth, it all sounded like a scam of some kind."

"Why Boston? What kind of treasure could be authenticated there?" Trout frowned. "She gave you no hint of what it might be?"

Sawyer followed Ginger down the stairs. "None."

"It clearly isn't in her room or she wouldn't have left it unlocked." Trout said as he followed Ginger and Sawyer back to the kitchen.

Ginger opened the pantry and took out a bottle of tequila. She poured three shots, cut a lime, and passed them around. Everyone threw back their shots and bit into the lime wedges.

"Better than coffee any day," Sawyer said. "Now tell me why everyone's so jumpy."

"It started with the dead body."

"That's always a good place to start." Sawyer said.

Ginger grinned, her lips began to tremble, then she started giggling. Tears rolled down her cheeks. Trout realized she was on the point of a real melt down.

"Maybe we should save the tall tales for another day, Sawyer." He went around the kitchen table and took Ginger in his arms and made shushing sounds. He sent Sawyer a look and the older man nodded and left the room.

Trout held her for a long time, gently swaying in a soothing motion until she became calm and lifted her head from his chest.

"I'm sorry," she sniffed. "I don't know where that came from."

"Over stressed, a sudden fright. It happens to the best of us."

"Not to me."

"Well, this time it did and that's okay. You're among friends."

She pulled free of his embrace, snatched a paper towel from the holder, and blew her nose. "God, I'm a mess."

"A little focus will help that. You have to let go of the things you can't control, and deal with the rest the best you can. Right now, we need to create a new system for guests coming and going."

"Since I don't appear to have any guests at the moment, it's the perfect opportunity," Ginger said and tried to smile.

"Agreed. Go take all the keys from the board and lock them in the registration desk drawer. The master keys as well. Keep the desk drawer key on a bungee cord on your wrist. You can pass it off to whoever's on duty. That way it's always under your control or that of one of your employees."

"Aye, aye, captain."

"First problem solved."

"And the next problem?" she asked.

"Call the bartender, what's his name? Harry?"

Ginger nodded.

"See if he can fill in for Jules for a few days. Until the convention guests arrive there won't be much demand on the bar and from what I can tell, he spends most of his time reading in the shade."

"He's a college student, but yeah, there's little for him to do other than keep the common areas tidy. I have to have someone out there from tea time forward. People on vacation don't want to have to track down someone to get them a drink when they're idling by the pool."

"Maybe Jules will be back by the time things get really busy.

Or Gabriella can give you a few more hours. It doesn't hurt to ask when you need help, Ginger."

"I know, I know, but it's hard for me. I've been trying to manage with as little help as possible. I need to clear enough profit to finish the garage apartment. That would give me extra rental income. It's ideal for someone living here, working in the tourist trade."

"That's good for the long term but right now we need to get through the coming week. Do what you gotta do."

"You're right. I guess I needed someone to tell me what I already knew."

"Good. All of this will get cleared up sooner or later. Sooner would be nice but for now the best way to cope is to focus on the here and now."

"You were good at your job."

Trout squeezed her hand. "It's the same advice anyone would give you. Now let's go see if Annette showed up for her meeting with Sawyer. One less missing guest would be a nice turn of events right now."

"While I was dusting I started thinking," Ginger said.

"About what?"

"There has to be a connection between Liberty and Annette. They checked into the B & B within a day of each other, they both came and went rather mysteriously, and someone tried to break into both their rooms in search of something."

"True.

THE MORNING SUN has reached my cozy little nesting place on the porch swing. I open my eyes, yawn, and stretch. There's nothing like a power nap when you've been on the job all night. It's still quiet on the streets of Key West. Here in the land of perpetual holiday no one stirs much before mid-morning except fishermen and joggers. What's up with that, anyway? The things humans will expend energy on.

By the sun's shadow I see that it's nearing ten o'clock. Time for even the most hung-over celebrant to be awake and stirring, even on a Sunday. I can't understand the appeal of total intoxication but it seems to be a favorite pastime of many tourists venturing to the southernmost tip of America, especially the young. I, for one, will guard my little gray cells from such a death but I confess that in my youth I was prone to hit the catnip pretty hard. That and a little bread pudding with whiskey sauce can still tempt me.

Thoughts of food send me in search of Ginger. It has been over two hours since the scone with jam. Delicious though it was, it's hardly enough nourishment for a working cat.

Trout is sleeping on the sofa in the sitting room. It's a well-deserved rest. I find he has proven himself by stepping into the trenches in Ginger's time of need. Well done, Trout. Ginger is polishing the registration desk. All the keys are gone from the board that usually houses them. Her level of activity suggests an almost manic need to regain control of her environment. I sympathize with her plight. There's nothing more worrisome than an unsolved murder on your home patch.

I hate to interrupt Ginger in her attack on the dust motes that dare reside at the Paradise so I think I'll do a walkabout of the premises, see that all is in order. The door of the Macaw Suite is closed. More's the pity. I would dearly love to get my paws on any evidence the Talents left behind. I'm in luck with the Bird Cage. Angela is changing the bed linens. There's a nice view of the pool from here. A light-filled room perfect for an escape from the hustle and bustle of the working world. I don't see why Liberty didn't like it.

Annette isn't a very tidy guest. She has shoes under the bed along with a bit of lacy undergarment. Her clothes are haphazardly hung in the armoire. Tsk-tsk, she's even left an uncapped fountain pen here on *the window seat and I'm afraid it has ruined the cushion. Ginger won't be pleased. And a sheet of old paper covered by scribbling and scratch outs is caught under the cushion. Annette has very poor penmanship. Maybe this is supposed to be French, but no, it is English. A name, Catherine. Hmmm. Gibberish.*

I had hoped for a clue as to why Annette came to Key West in the doldrums of summer but apparently she has shrugged off the chore that brought her here and is simply enjoying herself. This is the second time that she has stayed out all night. With whom, I wonder.

Ah, well, there's nothing to be learned here. After my nap, I begin to see there might be something to Megs' claims of Annette being a spy. Perhaps not a spy, per se, but up to something. It's amazing what a little sleep will do for the facile mind. I should find her and see if I can extract more pearls of wisdom from her babble. I'm sure she and Bartholomew can't be far.

TROUT WOKE WITH A START. He hadn't intended to fall asleep but rather to be on the look-out for Annette or the Talents. He could see Ginger tending the ferns on the porch. She had foresworn the usual tropical print wrap skirt she generally wore as mistress of the Paradise and had on a pair of crisp white shorts. When she tip-toed to reach the watering can to the ferns, her lovely legs were a sight to rouse any man from sleep.

With a yawn, he sat up and realized that he had been in the same clothes for going on three days. A shower and a shave were the order of the morning.

He went onto the porch and took the watering can from Ginger, refilling it at the spigot at the end of the porch. "No sign of anyone, I take it?"

"No. I changed out the key system like you suggested so

anyone returning is going to have to track me down to get into their rooms."

"How about Harry? Did you get up with him?"

"He'll be along in about thirty minutes, although I don't see why I'll need him until Wednesday."

"Annette might still return. She didn't make it back until almost two yesterday afternoon. I think she might have found something interesting to occupy her time."

"Maybe. She seemed so concerned about making her business contacts that it's hard for me to believe she wouldn't make the effort to be here for her meeting with Sawyer."

"You have a point," Trout said. He raised the can heavy with water up to the hanging ferns. "But as you keep saying, she's French." He gave the fern a good drenching. "You might not need Harry after today but I'm glad he's coming. I need to get back to the *Baby Buddha* and clean up a bit. You know what they say about fish, after three days, throw them out."

"Sorry, Trout. You've been a big help and it isn't fair of me to impose on you like this."

"Think nothing of it. I didn't have anything else to do."

"Don't worry about me. I'll manage from here." Ginger took the empty watering can. "I've seen the light and will call in the help I need."

"I'll be back tonight."

"Really, Trout..."

"Dinner would be nice. My cupboard is pretty bare."

Ginger hesitated. "Okay. But after I feed you and the cat, you're going home to get some real rest."

"See you about seven," he said and walked down the steps and away from the Paradise.

The streets were quiet as Trout made his way toward the marina. He stopped in at Sawyer's apartment and knocked.

There was no answer. It had occurred to Trout after Sawyer left the Paradise that it was odd Annette would come all the way to Key West to meet with someone she hadn't made some kind of prior connection with before such a costly venture. He tried to remember Sawyer's exact words when asked about their meeting. *She came to me*, he had said.

What difference did it make, Trout asked himself. The real mystery was who killed Liberty and why. Annette's little business venture or scam was beside the point. Or was it? Sawyer was a grown man, Trout reasoned. A pretty savvy one, too. He could take care of himself.

But why did someone break into Annette's room? There had to be a connection with Liberty, there just had to be. It was too much of a coincidence otherwise. Were the two women in cahoots?

Trout shook his head and climbed aboard the *Baby Buddha*, a shower foremost in his thoughts. He ducked into the cabin. It took a couple of seconds for his eyes to adjust to the dim light but immediately he knew he was in trouble. Someone had broken into his storage locker and pretty much trashed the boat. All the kitchen cabinets were hanging open. The door to the cubby was ajar and the bedding was on the floor. "Shit!"

He began to sort through his possessions. Whoever it was hadn't done as much damage as he first thought. Nothing was broken, just turned upside down in a very thorough search. When he found his wallet with nine one hundred dollar bills still in it, he knew they were after something else. The problem was Trout didn't own anything else of value. Three break-ins, or possibly four if someone really had been in Liberty's room the night she died. Someone was desperate to find whatever they were looking for, even to the point of trashing Trout's boat.

. . .

Ginger looked up from the computer at the registration desk to see a very large man climbing the front steps of the Paradise. He stopped when he gained the front porch and wiped his brow with a handkerchief. By the time he opened the door into the foyer, he was quite flushed. He brought with him the distinct scent of cigars.

"May I help you?" Ginger asked.

"Good afternoon," the man said. "I've been told by one of the local bartenders that the Paradise Bed and Breakfast has the best key lime pie in Key West. Is that true?"

Jerry's handiwork, Ginger thought, and perhaps Liberty's fat man. "Just about every establishment in the city lays claim to that distinction but I confess I think mine is the best."

"Well, then," he said, "I have come to try it. Do you make it yourself?"

"I do," Ginger smiled, "from my grandmother's recipe."

"Excellent," he said. "A tried and true family recipe is generally known to be superior to all these so-called delicacies that are mass produced in some cold sterile pie factory." He wiped his forehead again. "Is it too early to have a sample, with perhaps a cup of Earl Grey tea?"

"Not at all. The Paradise serves tea from three until five-thirty. Your timing is perfect." Ginger came from behind the registration counter. "If you'll follow me."

She sat him in the bay window of the dining room and brought him iced water. The poor man looked like he could use it. "How do you like your tea? Milk or lemon?"

"Milk, please. I've tried to like it with lemon but find my taste can't adapt, kind of like drinking gin and tonic in the winter."

"Around here gin and tonic in the winter isn't very different from the summer."

He laughed. "I see what you mean."

She brought him a pot of tea, properly steeped with boiling hot water, and a piece of her pie artfully embellished with a razor thin slice of lime.

"Are you the proprietress of this lovely establishment?" he asked.

"I am," she replied.

"It's rather a grand old house, isn't it?"

She realized he wanted someone to visit with. Many older people on their own quite often did. Was that why he had sat and talked with Liberty, she wondered. "Yes," she said. "It was built in 1900. My grandmother inherited it from her second husband and it's been in the family since."

"I can tell it has been lovingly preserved. As we get older I think we have an affinity with old things, don't you?"

"Perhaps."

"Ah, you're too young to have such nostalgic feelings but you will one day."

"I'm pretty attached to the old place. It's the only home I've ever known and it has many memories of my grandmother and mother." She hesitated then said, "I couldn't help but notice that you're a cigar smoker."

"One of my vices, I confess. I've run across a merchant on Wall Street who has some lovely handmade Arturo Fuente cigars. I apologize if my passion for them is offensive."

"No, not at all." Ginger poured him more tea. "I rather like the slightly sweet fragrance."

"You're very tolerant, dear child." He added milk to his tea and took a sip. "The perfect accompaniment to your pie. The bartender was correct, you know. This is the best key lime pie

I've tasted here or anywhere. I daresay the recipe is a highly guarded secret."

"Which bartender told you about the Paradise? I'd like to thank him."

"I don't know his name. He probably told me but, alas, I'm not always good about remembering. Except for pretty young women, of course. Every waiter these days introduces themselves and all those names quickly disappear like mist in the morning sun. But I remember he works at the Green Parrot."

"Probably Jerry."

"You know," he said, "I do believe that was his name. Had a British accent."

"Australian, actually. Would you like another piece of pie?"

"Thank you, no. The world is full of temptations so I try to savor them in small samples lest there be no room for others that will surely follow."

"A man of restraint."

He chuckled. "You wouldn't know it by the look of me, but I do try to contain my passions. There is always the unexpected treasure just behind the next door, so to speak."

"If I might be so forward as to ask, do you know a woman named Liberty Anderson?"

He looked at Ginger, cut his eyes upward as if trying to recall, then shook his head. "I don't think so. Where would I know her from, do you think?"

"The Green Parrot, maybe."

"Well, that could be. I've spent some time there in recent days. It's a lively place filled with young people. I like to be surrounded by all that energy and gaiety. One of the pleasures of being my age and having such a, ummm, robust figure, is that they are quite willing to indulge in conversation with me, harmless old man that I am. What does she look like?"

"Blond..."

"I'm partial to blonds. After redheads, of course."

Ginger smiled. "Life of the party," she continued, "red dress, very Marilyn Monroe."

"Oh, my, yes. Lovely girl. A bit tipsy but full of life." He frowned. "But I don't think her name was Liberty. That's a name that one would remember. It seems she called herself Stella. Maybe I have the wrong young woman, after all."

"Huh," Ginger gave a little shrug, "could be."

CHAPTER NINE

The lizard has become rather brazen. He doesn't even flinch when I pass by. Life in paradise seems to have inured him to his genetic sensibilities. He is safe from me. I haven't the time or inclination to toy with him.

I've seen no sign of Megs and Bartholomew. It would be nice to know who Megs thinks Annette is spying on, unless she has it all wrong and it's the other way around. Perhaps it's time I checked in on Mr. Fortesque. His agents, Ray and Crissy Talent, haven't returned to the Paradise since our encounter at Mallory Pier. I fear I've overplayed my hand and they know we are on to them.

People are still having breakfast on the porch of the Curry Mansion Inn. A lazy Sunday brunch is one of their calling cards, I believe. The aroma of several tempting dishes teases my palate but I must stay focused.

Fortesque, of necessity, I imagine, has a room on the ground floor. It doesn't open directly onto the swimming pool but close enough that my presence won't seem amiss to anyone who might notice. And what is this? His door is open. The maid's cart stands on the pathway outside but there is no sign of her. Am I a lucky black cat, or what? The bed is stripped so I know she will return soon. I must make quick work of the time I have. This worn leather attaché seems promising. Worn, perhaps, but very expensive leather. A highly polished brass nameplate affixed to the front says H. Fortesque. How fortuitous. Just a nudge of the paw, and, oh my, it tips over, spilling some of the contents. Documents, documents, stationary, postage stamps. The man has a veritable office with him. Let's see if anything here gives a glimmer of why he has come to Key West.

TROUT RAN a hand across his jaw and examined his face in the small rectangle of mirror in the tiny head of the *Baby Buddha*. Close enough, he decided. After a couple of hours sleep he was feeling himself again. The boat had been restored to order, his wallet now securely in his back pocket. He had donned his best old Hawaiian print shirt and his only pair of long pants. He wasn't sure why. It was just dinner with Ginger at the Paradise. *Right.*

He stopped by Sawyer's apartment when he left the pier. Still no one home. On a hunch, he decided to check in at the marina office. Mikey was there trying to fix a Penn Fierce II reel. It kept catching.

"Thought those were supposed to hold up under any kind of misuse," Trout said.

"Aye. They're supposed to."

Mikey wasn't in the best humor but then, he rarely was.

"Did you see anyone around the marina earlier?"

"Lots of people."

"Anyone who didn't look like they belonged?"

"How's that look?"

"Never mind," Trout said. "Do you know anyone who might be interested in taking on one of my charters?"

"Depends. When is this charter?" Mikey asked.

"Wednesday morning. Six o'clock."

Mikey looked out through the windows of the marina office along the long pier of docked boats. "Maybe J.J. He's got a new baby. Could probably use the extra cash." He glanced up at Trout. "Why? I thought you were broke."

"Taking a personal day," Trout said.

Mikey stared at him a long heartbeat then returned his to attention to the fishing reel.

"Know where I might find Sawyer?" Trout asked.

"Gone."

"Gone? Where?"

Mikey shrugged. "Don't know. Drove him into Miami about eleven."

"Where in Miami?"

Mikey looked up from the task in hand. "Why?"

"Curious." Trout said.

"Curiosity killed the cat."

"So they say."

"Uh huh."

"I don't suppose you dropped him at the airport?"

"Can't say."

"Right." Trout stood watching Mikey fish line from the reel. "Will he be back anytime soon?"

"What's the emergency?"

"Nothing. He missed an appointment with a woman at the Paradise. I'm headed that way. Seemed important at the time but maybe not."

"Maybe not."

It was obvious Mikey wasn't going to tell Sawyer's business. That was one reason Sawyer kept him close, Trout supposed. A good gofer is one who can keep your secrets.

Trout stepped out of the marina office and stood a moment enjoying the sun lowering in the western sky. The days were already getting shorter, little by little, but here in the land of forever summer the seasons didn't change much except for the hours of sunlight. He dreaded the coming of long winter nights. In the light of day it was so much easier to keep the shadows at bay.

He turned from the view and let his thoughts wander to Ginger of the Titian red hair. He had a decision to make. Perhaps it had already been made. Events seemed to be conspiring to throw them together. What he knew he had to do now was decide whether or not he would keep resisting. Or if he was still capable of doing so.

It was a peaceful walk along Duval Street at this hour. The only real activity was a couple in front of the Gold Empire convenience store checking their scratch offs to see if they were lottery winners. Trout was about to cross the street when the door of the Starbucks opened and Mel Anderson stepped out, a tall coffee in hand.

"Mrs. Anderson," he said.

She gave a start and looked up at him. "Mr..."

"Trout," he said.

"From the Paradise."

"I thought you'd be on your way back to DC by now."

"So did I, but apparently nothing happens in this sauna of a hell-hole on the week-end."

"What seems to be the problem?"

"Arty. They won't let me have him."

"Why?"

"Bureaucracy. What else?"

"Well, maybe they'll be able to sort things out tomorrow."

"You've obviously never worked for the government."

Trout made no comment.

"Monday's the day everyone spends getting over the week-end. Nothing gets done."

"Speaking from experience, are you?" Trout suppressed the urge to laugh.

It was Mel's turn to be uncommunicative.

"Things might be different this time," Trout said.

"Hello?" she said. "Do you even know where you are?"

Trout grinned. Mel was probably right.

"This place is costing me a fortune. If that hussy wasn't already dead, I'd kill her."

"Huh. Well, good luck with the authorities."

Mel nodded and set off in the direction from which he had come.

Duncan would have been smart to give her the ashes, Trout thought as he continued along Duval Street.

He was greeted by the smell of red meat searing on hot metal when he rounded the corner of the bed and breakfast and crossed the lawn to an outdoor kitchen near the back entrance into the Paradise.

"This is a rare treat," he said as Ginger looked up from the grill.

She smiled. "I decided we could both use a little boost of iron."

"Can I help?"

"Open the wine so it can breathe. Everything else is ready."

"You shouldn't have gone to so much effort."

"It's all easy enough; steak, salad, fruit. How do you like your steak?"

"Medium rare." He said as he took the corkscrew to the bottle of red wine. The cork came out with a satisfying pop.

"Medium rare it is," Ginger said as she turned the meat and offered up her glass.

Trout poured for both of them. "How'd your afternoon go?"

"Interesting," she said then told him about the visit from the fat man.

"You think it's the same guy from the Green Parrot?"

"It'd be hard to imagine two men fitting that description being in Key West at the same time."

"Agreed." Trout savored the red wine. Ginger knew her stuff. The steaks were resting under aluminum foil while she tossed the salad.

"Do you believe him about coming to the Paradise for pie?"

"It would be a strange coincidence even though Jerry has been talking things up for me."

"And you don't believe in coincidences."

"Exactly."

"What do you think he wanted?" Trout asked.

"I'm as puzzled as you are. The conversation was nothing but small talk. He freely admitted seeing Liberty or someone who fit her description. He talked about life's pleasures and his vices. Nothing specific other than cigars and pie but there was a sense of expectation, as if he was waiting for something."

"Did you think he was fishing for information?"

"Not that I could tell."

"Odd."

"Very." She plated the salad. "How was your afternoon? Get any sleep?"

"You could say it was equally eventful."

"How so?"

"Someone broke into the *Baby Buddha* and trashed the place."

"Oh, Trout! No!" Ginger's hand went to her throat. She had a stricken look on her face.

"No real damage but a very thorough search."

"What did they take?"

"Nothing that I could tell." He felt reassuringly of his back pocket. "They left behind a lot of expensive fishing gear and my pocket change."

"What were they after?"

"Good question."

"Do you think it was simply for the sake of mischief? An act of vandalism?"

"No."

"It has to be connected to what's going on here."

"That's what I'm thinking."

She placed the salad plates on the small bistro table by the pool. It was laid with fresh white linens and held a small bouquet of daisies. Trout refilled their wine glasses and placed them on the table.

They moved the conversation to other things while they enjoyed their meal, the renovation of the garage apartment, the dread of Fantasy Fest and all the madness and debauchery it would bring at the end of October. The event was a double-edged sword. The Paradise was always full but the clientele tended to be out of control for a span of ten days. Ginger and all her staff would be run off their feet.

The steak Ginger served Trout was enough meat for a man twice his size but he made good headway with it. When he sat back in his chair and drained the last of the wine from his glass, he said, "You're one hell of a good cook, Ginger."

"Anyone can throw a piece of meat on a fire."

"Take the compliment. It's well deserved. It isn't just the steak, or the right wine, it's all the little details, all the time and energy you spend on everything to make your business a success. You should be proud of all you've accomplished."

Ginger blushed and looked away from his steady gaze. "I'm always comparing myself to my mother. Or my grandmother. For them everything was always effortless and everyone who came to the Paradise had the most wonderful experiences. Many of them came back year after year." She shrugged. "Mom and Gran had an ease about them, you know? People felt like family or old comfortable friends."

"I feel that way. I'm sure your guests do too."

Trout could see that the personal nature of the conversation was making Ginger uncomfortable. She said, "Speaking of guests, there's been no sign of Annette or Ray and Crissy Talent. I called Duncan to see if he wanted to finger print their room before I cleaned it but he already has a set from the initial break-in. They're not in any criminal data base so there's that at least. I'm leaving everyone's things in place tonight but tomorrow I'm packing it all up." She shifted in her chair. "I'm beginning to worry about Annette."

"Me too."

"Duncan said he'd have the patrols keep an eye out for her. She's not officially missing yet. It's been less than twenty-four hours. He's going to run her passport and see if he can learn anything helpful."

"It occurred to me that neither of us saw her leave last night. She came back to the Paradise because she broke the heel off her shoe. That was early evening. I went to the hospital with Jules and you dealt with the police and locked up. We assumed she was in her room all that time because her key wasn't on the board."

"I've worried with that all afternoon. She could easily have left while I cleaned the coffee spill and print powder from the pantry. For some reason I just assumed she wouldn't go out after the fright she had."

"Maybe the incident spooked her, especially after what happened to Liberty."

"But where would she go?" Ginger asked.

"I don't know. Another hotel, maybe."

"Possibly, but she left all her things."

"No one is behaving as they should," Trout said with a sigh.

GINGER LOOKED AROUND at the rustling coming from the cast iron plants. Trouble strolled from the foliage and came to inquire about his dinner. She smiled. "Where are your side-kicks?" she asked.

The cat looked up at her with an expression that she could have sworn said, *Oh, please.*

"Do you ever get the impression he knows what we're saying?" she asked Trout.

"Actually, I get the feeling he thinks we haven't a clue about anything."

"Well," she said, "he is a cat."

"Meaning?"

"They know they're superior and love toying with us."

"If you say so."

"Ever read *Old Possums Book of Practical Cats?*" The cat's ears twitched.

"Nope. But I saw the play."

"Yeow." Trouble said.

"Well?" Ginger asked.

"I think Eliot had too much time on his hands."

"Men." Ginger said and smiled as she stood to do Trouble's bidding. "I hope you like your steak medium rare, and a bit cold." She took their leftovers to the outdoor kitchen area and cut some of Trout's T-bone into small bits. "Tammy Lynn is going to scold both of us if you put on too much weight while she's gone."

The cat seemed unconcerned about the possibility of a scolding. As soon as Ginger placed the scraps of meat on a bread and butter plate on the brick pavers beside the grill, he tucked into it with gusto.

Ginger returned to the table and helped Trout gather the remaining dishes and cutlery. They took them into the kitchen and began to wash up.

As Trout dried the wine glasses and returned them to the china cabinet, Ginger went through to the foyer and found Harry reading a textbook. "All quiet?" she asked.

Harry sat back on the high stool behind the registration desk and nodded.

"You might as well go on home. It looks like it's an empty house tonight. No need for you to have a restless night on the daybed."

"You're sure?" Harry asked.

Ginger nodded. "I'll take the key."

Harry took the bungee cord from his wrist and gave it to Ginger. "You need me to come in tomorrow morning? I don't have a class until eleven."

"No," Ginger sighed. "All that needs doing will be cleaning the Bird Cage and the Macaw Suite. I can handle that. Angela has the day off tomorrow as well. But I'll need you back at one on Wednesday. The conventioneers should be arriving by then."

"Cool." Harry collected his book and cell phone and strolled out the front door of the Paradise.

Ginger placed the door on auto lock and dimmed the lights

on the front porch. When she entered the kitchen, Trout had stored the leftovers in the refrigerator and wiped down the work table. He was drying the kitchen sink.

He looked up from this task and said, "What next?"

"Nothing. There's no need to do the breakfast set-up. It would be a waste of food and effort. If Annette shows up before morning I can handle whatever she might need easy enough." She frowned. "I wonder if Sawyer ever caught up with her."

"I don't think so. He left town right after he was here."

"Where'd he go?"

"Mikey wouldn't say but I'd suspect he went to Boston."

"Because that's where Annette went before coming to Key West. To get authentication."

"I also think Sawyer has an idea of what Annette is hawking. It must be something of serious value for him to take off like that."

"Boston is a maritime city like Key West. Perhaps it has to do with ships and sunken treasure after all."

"We won't know until one of them shows up and spills the beans." Trout said.

"You're right." She looked around the tidy kitchen. "Thanks, Trout. Not just for this but for everything. I know you didn't want to be drawn into this mess..."

Trout came around the table and took Ginger's hand. "I'm glad I was here."

"Me too," she said and looked up into his pale blue eyes. "I sent Harry home. There was no need for him to ..."

"Ginger," Trout slowly drew her into his arms and kissed her.

. . .

FINALLY, Trout and Ginger have stopped dancing around the inevitable. The only problem with that is they'll be distracted in a major way. Not that I can't handle this case on my own but an opposable thumb would come in handy at the moment. I'll leave them to it. I need to figure out how to get into the Bird Cage. This business of spilled beans is enlightening. The king of the conchs is looking to buy something from Annette Benoit. If Megs' ramblings are anything to go by, I'll bet my whiskers that Annette was originally intended to occupy the Toucan Suite. I need to get back into both rooms.

GINGER MADE a small carafe of coffee and poured a cup. She went to stand at the kitchen window overlooking the back grounds of the Paradise. For the first time in days, she felt at peace. With no guests at the bed and breakfast she could be leisurely.

"Good morning," Trout said from the doorway to the hall.

Ginger turned and smiled. "Morning."

He crossed the room to where she stood. "Smells good," he said, then he took her cup, set it on the window sill, and kissed her.

He was a good kisser. A very good kisser. The nice thing about good kisses, Ginger thought, was that they led to other very nice things. "How'd you sleep?" she asked.

"Seriously?"

She smiled more broadly and he kissed her again.

"Breakfast?" she asked when he finally broke the kiss.

"Might be a good idea," he said and grinned. "Before I get a better idea."

Ginger felt the blush all over her body. "Probably a good idea," she agreed. "It's a work day, after all."

"You always get up this early?"

"That's the life," she said. "Usually I'm baking something fresh for my guests by now. In fact, I feel like a sluggard this morning. I don't know when I last had a free morning."

"You should hire more help."

"That's a luxury only the bigger establishments can afford. The house is old, the upkeep high, and people are accustomed to five star service these days."

"Ever think of doing anything else? Something less demanding?"

"I won't deny it's crossed my mind once or twice. But it's what I know and, as you reminded me last night, I'm good at it. My mother once told me that a man's arms around you always felt good, but a man and his embrace came and went. The Paradise would always be here."

"Sounds like your mother was a wise woman."

"Life does that to you, I guess."

"What about your father? Or were his the arms that came and went?"

"A psychologist, huh?"

"Sorry."

"It's okay. I get my red hair from him. Sailor Sam. My mother always referred to him that way. Not my husband or your father, just Sailor Sam. He was with the naval base when they met and married but like the tide, he came and went. He was stationed in Guam, Hawaii, California for a while."

"Your mother didn't move with him?"

"No. Gran needed her here and I don't think she really wanted to go. Maybe she realized early on that he couldn't stay and she couldn't leave."

"What happened to him?"

"I don't know." Ginger went to the coffee pot and refilled her cup. She took down a clean one for Trout and filled it as well. "He used to turn up once in a while when I was little but at some point he stopped."

"Did they divorce?"

"No. I don't think so. You have to remember my mother and grandmother were conchs. Life down here isn't the same as the mainland. No one worries too much about the formalities. I suppose he could be anywhere. He could be dead."

"You have no desire to find out?"

"No. I never knew him and between my grandmother and my mother, I never needed him. I suppose I would have turned out differently if I'd had a father but maybe not."

"What would you have done differently, do you think?"

Ginger shrugged. "Gotten married I suppose. I came close. He was from Iowa."

"Iowa?" Trout grinned. "I can't picture you in Iowa."

Ginger arched and eyebrow and smiled. "Why ever not?"

"Maybe it's the red hair. I don't think it would work anywhere but here, against all this green foliage. And the brown eyes, very tropical."

"Funny man."

"Your mother must have lived a lonely life if he disappeared when you were young."

"I didn't say my mother was alone. Men came into her life and, I guess you could say, her arms. They came and they went but it wasn't a strife filled coming and going. As I said, she and my grandmother had an ease about them. They embraced the life they had and were content."

"Next you'll be telling me things about your grandmother that would make me blush."

"She was married three times. She buried the first two, my grandfather, then her second husband who left her the Paradise, although at the time it was her home, not a bed and breakfast. The third one wandered off to the mainland and never returned."

"That must have been hard on you as a kid."

Her forehead creased with frown lines for a brief moment then she shook her head. "I don't remember Gran's last husband. And I suppose because I was a child, I didn't appreciate the significance of the men who came to stay with my mother for a while then disappear. This is Key West, after all. But when I was in junior high I went home with a friend from school to stay overnight. I heard Alice's mother and grandmother talking in the kitchen while they prepared dinner. That's when I realized my home life was different."

"How did that make you feel?"

Ginger shrugged. "It obviously made an impression or I wouldn't have remembered it. I can't say it changed me or my attitude toward my circumstances. Or maybe it did. Maybe that's why I almost married Mr. Iowa." She smiled but it quickly faded. "I never felt like I fit on the mainland. It was like I was out of synch with everyone around me."

Ginger realized she'd said too much. She turned to the bread box, opened it, and busied herself with finding the freshest of the croissants. "Anyway, those are the facts. Just so you know," she said, her back to Trout.

Trout came to the counter where she worked and took the bread from her hands. He turned her so she faced him. "I was married," he said. "Twice." With that he took her by the hand. "Just so you know." Then he led her out of the kitchen and down the hallway toward the back of the Paradise.

TROUT AND GINGER stood in the open doorway to the Bird

Cage. No one had touched it since Angela made up the bed the previous morning.

"You're sure about this?" he asked.

"Her reservation ended with the eleven o'clock check-out today. She's been gone nearly forty-eight hours. I don't know what else to do. Besides, I have guests for every room in the place on Wednesday."

"Okay. Where should we start?"

"Well, the bed is fine. There are clean towels in the bathroom. I suppose I just need to pack up her things, dust, and make sure there's nothing in the bathroom."

Trout ducked into the bathroom and brought out a flimsy robe. "It was on the hook on the back of the door."

Ginger took the suitcase from the bottom of the armoire and opened it on the bed. "Everything in here, I guess. I'll keep it in storage." She started gathering the items on the dressing table. One of the pots of cream was open. She lifted it to her nose and inhaled, closing her eyes as she did. "Expensive stuff," she said. Then she screwed the lid on and placed it in the suitcase.

Along with her clothing, shoes, and unmentionables, there was a valise. Ginger was hesitant to look inside but Trout wasn't so squeamish.

"An iPad," he said, "some business cards..."

"What do they say?"

He turned one toward the window for better light. "Annette Benoit, d'Agents Littéraire, and a phone number. Foreign, odd sequence, probably France," he said.

"Agent of what? You think that means literature?"

"I don't speak French but that would be my guess."

"Here," she held out her hand and Trout placed the card in

it. "I'll call the number when we finish and see what we can learn."

Trout placed the suitcase of Annette's belongings in the hallway and took a feather duster to the top of the highboy and the posters on the bed.

Ginger laughed. "If you could see yourself. All you need is a short black skirt and a white apron and cap."

"One of your favorite fantasies, I suppose?"

"My favorite fantasy is a maid, regardless of black skirt and apron, to do this every day for free."

"While you lounge by the pool eating bonbons and sipping champagne, no doubt. Well, madam, your wish is my command," he said with an awkward curtsy.

Ginger shook her head and turned to the window seat. She snatched up the cushion and swore under her breath.

"What?" Trout asked.

She held up a pretty pillow covered in a tropical print chintz. "Ink all over the cushion. It's ruined." She felt along the wooden structure of the seat and found the uncapped pen. "I really loved this pattern."

"It wasn't a cherished heirloom, was it?"

"No." She sighed. "And I've had worse things happen. I'm still sometimes amazed what total intoxication can make a normal person think is reasonable behavior." She took the pillow to the laundry cart and stacked it on top of the waste bin.

As she turned back into the room she glimpsed a tiny corner of paper under the bed. She bent down and retrieved it. Also lurking beneath the bed was a pair of sandals and some lacy panties. She made a note to herself to speak to Angela and Gabriella about the meaning of the words *thorough* cleaning.

The shoes and undergarment went into the suitcase. After a quick glance at the piece of paper, she added it to the trash.

With one last check of the bathroom, she said, "That does it, I think."

As Ginger locked the room, Trout glanced down the hallway to the emergency escape window. There on the landing were the two Hemingway cats, Lou Costello and Mitzy Gaynor. "I think those two have taken up residence at the Paradise."

Ginger followed the direction of his gaze. "They have been around a lot lately. It's unusual to see them so often but maybe that's because of Trouble. Curiosity killed the cat."

Trout stood there staring. Something about the phrase niggled at the back of his mind. What was it that this image was trying to trigger? The two cats sat there staring back at him.

CHAPTER TEN

I top the stairs to the fire escape window of the Paradise and find Megs and Bartholomew staring into the building. "I've been looking for you two," I say.

"Why?" Bartholomew asks.

"I need to know why Megs thinks Annette is a spy, and I need to get into the Bird Cage."

"You just missed your chance," Megs says.

I look into the window and catch a glimpse of the maid's cart being pushed around the corner and out of sight of the Bird Cage by Trout. I realize I've dallied too long at the museum checking out Hemingway's writing studio. The forces surrounding the murder at the Paradise are gathering and I needed to be sure of my facts.

"How did you know Annette was a spy?" I ask Megs.

"She hides things."

"What things?"

"Black things."

"With red trim," Bartholomew adds.

"How do you know she hides things?"

"We watch," Megs says.

"What do these things look like?" I ask.

"Not too big," Bartholomew says.

"And not too small," Megs says.

I want to bash my head against the window. Instead I ask, "Bigger than a breadbox?"

"What's a breadbox?" she wants to know.

I search my memory for something a cat could relate to. "Is it like your bed cushion?"

"I don't know," Megs replies, "I haven't slept on it."

This is pointless. I'll have to go with my hypothesis and see where that gets me. Megs and Bartholomew aren't going to be any help.

I hear a car door slam and I look toward the street. The fat man, H. Fortesque, to be more precise, has just emerged from a stretch limousine and is making his way to the front porch of the Paradise. Interesting, most interesting. I hasten down the stairs and in through the back door of the bed and breakfast.

By the time H. Fortesque reaches the foyer of the Paradise, I'm sitting, waiting, anxious to see what brings the mountain to Paradise.

GINGER HEARD the closing of the front door and came down the stairs to find the connoisseur of key lime pie standing in the foyer mopping his brow with a handkerchief.

"Hello. Again," she said. "Back for more pie?"

He smiled and angled his head a bit in a bashful acknowledgment that she wasn't fooled by his subterfuge. "Ms. Browne," he said in a winded voice. "You'll forgive me while I catch my breath. Exertion is no friend to a fellow of my physique, especially in this climate."

Ginger motioned with her hand toward the sitting room. "Please, come have a seat."

"Thank you." He followed her into the spacious, light filled room and wisely took the center of a loveseat.

"Can I get you anything? A glass of water?"

"That would be lovely."

As Ginger turned toward the foyer, Trout strolled into the room.

"Hello." He came to a stop a few feet from where the fat man sat.

"Good afternoon." Fortesque mopped his forehead once again with the handkerchief. "August is not the ideal month to visit Key West, is it?"

"Depends," Trout said, "on why you're here."

He chuckled. "Right to the point. I like that." He offered Trout his hand and as they shook, he said, "Heronimous Fortesque at your service."

"Armentrout Richardson."

Fortesque inclined his head. "Admirable name."

"Likewise."

Ginger appeared on the tail end of this exchange with the glass of water. "What can we do for you, Mr. Fortesque?"

He took a long drink of the water and placed the glass on the side table. "That was refreshing. Thank you." He looked from Ginger to Trout. "I'm here to see Ms. Benoit."

"The literary agent." Ginger said on a hunch.

"Ah. So you know the story."

"Why don't you tell us your version," Trout said.

A look of cunning appeared in Fortesque's eyes. "Where is Ms. Benoit?"

"She's not here at the moment," Ginger said. *He knows we're fishing*, she thought. "She missed her other appointment as well," she added in the hope it would appear they knew more about what was going on.

"So Ray was right," Fortesque said.

"About what?" Trout asked.

"The other bidder."

"Where are Ray and Crissy Talent, Mr. Fortesque?" Ginger asked.

He smiled. "I imagine they're happily counting their good fortune in a little bungalow off Flagler. It was easier to pay them off than allow them to proceed in their blundering way and risk drawing attention to the negotiations."

"You mean alerting someone like the other cigar aficionado, you mean?"

For an instant Trout thought he had caught Fortesque off guard. But just as quickly the fat man regained his composure.

Fortesque openly assessed Trout. After a long pause he said. "Ah. Has Ms. Benoit met with this other," he waved his hand as if summoning the word he wanted from the air, "collector."

"Is that what you are?" Trout asked. "A collector."

"Didn't Ms. Browne tell you?"

"She said you liked pie."

Fortesque laughed. "Yes, I like pie. I like many things."

"Old things," Ginger said. "Treasures that tempt you, that's your passion, isn't it?"

Fortesque tilted his head slightly in acknowledgement.

"What were Ray and Crissy Talent doing for you, Mr. Fortesque? Are those their real names?"

Fortesque's brows shot up in a look of amusement. "Does it really matter?"

"Detective Moore thinks so. Murder is serious business." Trout said.

Fortesque tut-tutted Trout and Ginger. "No one could seriously think those two capable of murder. Ineptitude certainly, but not murder."

"We know they were in Liberty Anderson's room and that she was murdered. Inept or not, that's pretty damning." Trout said.

"They also lured her away from the Chart Room Bar when she was too drunk to resist." Ginger added.

"This is all very melodramatic," Fortesque said. "How can you possibly know it was them? The truth of the matter is that the unfortunate dead woman has nothing to do with me or my associates." He saw the look on Ginger's face. "Yes, yes, I know about the woman who died in one of your rooms. The whole island knows. She has nothing to do with my business here."

"What is your business, Mr. Fortesque?" Trout asked.

Fortesque smiled. "Private. And it will stay that way until I've met with Ms. Benoit. After that, I'll be happy to tell your Detective Moore all about the miscreant Talents. They're harmless bumblers but I'll let him find that out for himself. Now," he said as he gathered himself to rise from the love seat, "I'll be on my way." When he had regained his balance he turned to Ginger and said, "Be so kind as to tell Ms. Benoit I called in when she returns."

With that he made his way to the foyer and out the door of the Paradise.

"WHAT DO YOU MAKE OF THAT," Trout asked Ginger as they watched Fortesque climb into the limousine.

"One of Mr. Fortesque's vices is rare things of great value and importance. Since Ms. Benoit's a literary agent, that suggests a rare old book of some kind, possibly one of

Hemingway's books since a number of people interested in what she has to offer have descended on Key West."

"Like a first edition?"

"Maybe. But all this secrecy suggests something more than that," Ginger said.

"And I know just the man to ask," Trout said. He gave Ginger a solid kiss and left the Paradise.

He hadn't gone two blocks when he realized the black cat was following him. Trout thought briefly that Ginger might worry about Trouble straying then laughed. The cat had a mind and will of his own. What Ginger wanted didn't figure into the equation. Just then he saw Mel Anderson coming out of the First Bank of the Florida Keys and stopped in his tracks. She was counting money which she then stuffed into her purse.

"Huh." He said to the cat. "Wonder what she's still doing in Key West?" Then he remembered her complaint about the difficulty of getting anything done with government bureaucracy on a Monday and smiled. Crusty old bat probably deserved the aggravation and expense, he decided.

With a shake of his head he walked on to the marina. Mikey was just coming out of the office when Trout climbed the steps.

"The boss back yet?"

Mikey jerked his head in the direction of the office door and continued on down the steps.

The bell over the door jangled when Trout opened it. Sawyer Daniels looked up from his computer screen at the sound and grinned. "Yo, Trout. Heard you were looking for me."

"How was Boston?" Trout asked.

Sawyer grinned more broadly. "Couldn't really say."

Trout let his gaze travel around the very club like surroundings of the marina office. A glass case contained an old boat captain's cap. Three shot glasses held pride of place before a photograph of Ernest Hemingway, Joe Russell, and a huge black man. "Who's the big guy?" Trout asked.

"Big Skinner," Sawyer said and leaned his chair back, his hands clasped behind his head. "Bartender at the Blind Pig. That would be Russell's first saloon after the end of Prohibition, before it became Sloppy Joe's and long before it changed locations."

There was a second photograph of Hemingway on a boat, probably the Pilar, Trout thought. "I hadn't realized you were such a fan of Hemingway." He looked from the photographs to Sawyer. "I've never seen you crack the spine of a book."

"It's not about the books, it's about the man." Sawyer rose from his chair and came to look at the photographs with Trout. "If I'd been around when they sold the house after his death, I'd have beaten Bernice Dickson to it."

Trouble wended his way between Sawyer's legs. "Got yourself a boat cat, huh?"

"No, he followed me from the Paradise. Belongs to Ginger's friend." Trout jangled the change in his pocket. "What did you find out at the JFK Library?"

Sawyer was silent for a minute then shook his head. "You're a nosy cuss, Trout. It's not good to meddle in other people's business."

"Ginger's in trouble. The whole island is talking about the death in the Paradise. The place is empty."

"What happened to the Benoit woman?"

"That's your concern? I thought you said Ginger was good people."

"She is, and nothing bad is going to happen to her or the

Paradise except they'll probably add her to the ghost tours'
route. That's not necessarily a bad thing, you know."

"What's the Benoit woman fencing?"

"Let's call it a silent auction, huh?" Sawyer went back to his
desk and leaned back in his chair, eyeing Trout.

Trouble jumped onto the desktop.

"It's all hush, hush," Sawyer said. "Supposedly someone
approached her with a lost piece of personal property that
belonged to Hemingway from his days on the continent."

"She's a literary agent. It doesn't take an Einstein to figure
out it has something to do with his writing." Trout moved to
the desk and scratched the cat's ears. "Did she say how she
came to have this object in her possession?"

"No real specifics, only that the source could be reliably
confirmed as having possession of it in a manner that's
realistic."

"What did you find out in Boston?"

Sawyer eyed Trout, gave a solitary shake of his head and
said, "That it's possible but highly improbable."

"What is it?"

"Don't know for sure."

"But you went looking for confirmation of something
specific so you have to have a pretty good idea."

"I do, Trout, but I'm not sharing. Not right now. After I
meet with Ms. Benoit, then we'll see. The truth of the matter
is that I'm still leaning heavily toward this being an elaborate
scam."

"What do you know about Liberty Anderson? What does
she have to do with all this?"

"Nothing. Duncan said it was a date rape thing gone south.
There'll be a manslaughter charge in it at the very least if they
can find who did it."

"You haven't had anyone snooping around the Paradise, have you?"

Sawyer's voice was sharp when he answered. "I wouldn't do that to Ginger."

"Do you know Fortesque?"

"The fat man? Yeah, I know him. We've crossed paths in the past."

"Is he capable of pushing the envelope as far as murder?"

"I wouldn't think so but I don't know. Besides, the dead woman has nothing to do with what we've got going on."

"I think she was killed by mistake."

Sawyer sat up straighter in his chair. "You think someone was after Annette Benoit?"

"That's the only thing that fits the facts so far. They're both blond, rather flamboyant, and they arrived at the Paradise within a day of each other. I think someone got them confused."

"Do you think whoever it was got what they were after?"

"I don't know. Annette is missing. There's been no sign of her for nearly forty-eight hours. Yet you're still here and so is Mr. Fortesque, both still eager to find Annette and her highly lucrative artifact. Could someone else be after the same item?"

"There's always that possibility."

"Any idea who the Cuban is?"

Sawyer hesitated. "I couldn't say for sure. There's one possibility. Geraldo Mechoso. His grandfather worked on the Hemingway farm, *Finca Vigia*, in Cuba. Ernesto, Geraldo's grandfather, would tell stories of Hemingway and the children. This was when Hemingway was married to his third wife, Martha. Geraldo supposedly has some correspondence from their friendship. It's rumored that he also has an early draft of *For Whom the Bell Tolls* but it's just that, rumor."

"Would he be in the running for this mysterious treasure Annette is trying to sell?"

"I doubt it. He has a cigar factory and does all right but not the kind of money he would need for something like this."

"Whatever this is," Trout said.

Sawyer just grinned. He sat forward in his chair, his forearms resting on the desktop. "Besides, he has a lot of other expenses. His daughter is vying for a place on the US Olympics team as a gymnast. She's good. Very good. But all that training and travel takes a lot of money." He hesitated then said, "It could be he thinks he can sell some of his grandfather's letters to Ms. Benoit. That would make more sense if you ask me."

I NOW KNOW the what of this Gordian Knot. A rare lost manuscript has supposedly surfaced. At least, that's what Annette is trying to auction off to a pack of avid collectors. There are plenty of sources to document Hemingway's writing life. From what I gather, so much of his writing is quasi autobiographical and that makes it easy to follow the progression of his career. What then could she possibly have that hasn't already been published or documented? Nothing. I believe Ms. Benoit to be a con artist.

Be that as it may, if the con is believed, then there might be someone out there who wants what she's offering badly enough to kill her for it. Two victims for different motives in the same place at the same time defies the laws of probability. That means either they're in cahoots on this caper or one of these women is an unintended victim. Which one is it?

Trout thinks it's Liberty. He's right in that no motive for her death has surfaced except an attempt at date rape, a rape that did not occur. Could something have scared the rapist off? I have to concede that's a possibility and that Liberty's death is the tragic accidental overdose it appears to be. Then why was Mechoso in her room?

We need to find Geraldo Mechoso. He has a hand in this, of that I'm sure. The scent of cigars has been the calling card for each intrusion into the Paradise and I can't think that it's our fat man.

Could Mechoso have followed Liberty thinking she was the literary agent? I can see how drugging her would facilitate a search of her room but how did he get in and out? If he accompanied her back to the Paradise he could have gone up with her with no one to witness it. But how to leave without the key being on the wrong side of the locked door? If the Talents were in the employ of H. Fortesque, and the center room, the Flamenco Suite, was occupied by the Williamsons, how did he escape?

THE MORNING HAD BEEN a wonderful interlude in the midst of all that was going on at the Paradise but now Ginger felt unsettled by the visit from Fortesque. On the surface, it appeared that two separate things had happened at the bed and breakfast in a short window of time. Liberty had been poisoned by a person or persons unknown for reasons unknown. Duncan thought she was the intended victim of an attempt at date rape. There was no physical evidence that a rape had occurred.

The second incident was the arrival of Annette Benoit from France by way of Boston, Massachusetts. What information had she been seeking there? Fortesque had hired the Talents to follow her. Were they responsible for the attempt to break into the Toucan Suite as well? If so was it as Fortesque said, that they were incompetent. Could this have led them to break into the wrong room? Did one of them actually succeed in gaining access to Annette's room? If not, then who had done those things sending first her then Jules to the hospital?

More and more it seemed to Ginger that the two women had some connection. How to find that connection was the problem.

She needed to let Duncan know the Talents were local. If he could pick them up for questioning they might get some answers to these questions. Until then there was no way to know how or if Liberty's death was connected to the missing literary agent. But one thing was certain in Ginger's mind. Two such mysterious events couldn't be a coincidence, especially in light of the fact that Annette was missing.

Ginger remembered the business card and dug it out of her back pocket. She started to dial the number with her cell phone then hesitated. What to say to whoever answered, she wondered. The best approach, she decided, was to act knowledgeable about Annette's business in Key West. Maybe her secretary would let something slip.

After a long silent few seconds, the number from Annette's business card began to ring. It was a short-lived victory. The second ring activated her voice mail and Ginger received a greeting in French. She supposed it was a request that she leave a message so she did. Only time would tell if this would get a response.

Worrying at all these loose threads of fact and speculation was giving her a headache. Make a list, she decided, a grocery list of last minute items for the incoming on Wednesday. She always found that a distraction freed the mind to seek its own answers.

Breakfast wouldn't be necessary on the first day of the convention but oranges for fresh juice and mimosas for the new arrivals were a must. Other fruits for the rooms, cheeses for tea time. She'd need to do some baking. She checked the refrigerator. Cream, of course. Champagne? The wine cooler held several bottles so she scratched it off the list.

Ginger's head snapped up and she stared out the kitchen window. *Ask Chink?* Those were the words scribbled in the corner of the marked up, scratched through, sheet of paper in Annette's room. She ran upstairs and threw open the door to the Bird Cage then remembered. She had thrown it in the trash.

The maid's cart was stashed in the large utility closet on the second floor. Ginger tossed the ruined seat cushion to the floor and found what she was looking for. The old, yellowed sheet of notebook paper lay on top of the waste bin. She retrieved it and looked at it closely. If this was what she thought it was, then she was on the trail of a real treasure and perhaps the key to the mystery of Liberty's death. The question was, how did one fit with the other?

She debated about whether or not to call Duncan and decided against it. He was already annoyed with her for interfering in the case. There was nothing to show that Liberty's death was anything other than an overdose of alcohol and GHB. No one was going to kill her over her investigation into the welfare of the Hemingway cats. To Ginger's knowledge, Duncan hadn't yet found a relative of any kind to claim her body. The truth was, no one cared enough about Liberty one way or the other to kill her. Unless, of course, she was involved in whatever brought Annette to Key West.

Ginger took the piece of paper to the window of the Bird Cage and looked at it in the bright light. What she needed to do was determine what she had. She went downstairs to her quarters and booted up her laptop.

For the next thirty minutes she searched the vast internet

for facts to support her theory. There was so much information on the subject of Hemingway that she felt overwhelmed. She sat back in her chair and wondered how to get to the crux of the matter. After a moment she stood, slipped the page of notebook paper into a file folder, and set off for the Hemingway Home Museum.

She did the whole tour of the house and the grounds, checked out the pet cemetery where past Hemingway cats were buried, saw their cat houses, and walked around the pool that Hadley, Hemingway's first wife, spent so much money to have dug.

When the press of tourists who had purchased tickets when she did had moved on she slipped into Hemingway's writing room and opened the file folder. Beside the old Royal Quiet Deluxe typewriter was a notebook staged as if the author was typing from the notes in it. She held the sheet of paper up to the words in the notebook and her heart began to race. Quickly she closed the file and turned to leave the room. Standing in the doorway was the nerdy Cary Grant.

"Hello," he said.

Ginger felt as if she'd been caught in a criminal act. She swallowed. "Hello. Again."

He smiled. "You remember."

"You were looking for Liberty Anderson."

His smile faded. "I heard the news. I didn't know."

"Have you talked to the police?"

He frowned. "Should I?"

"They've been trying to establish her activities since she arrived in Key West. I'm sure they'd like to know how you met her."

He nodded then with his forefinger pushed his glasses up onto the bridge of his nose. "I hadn't thought of that." He gave a slight shrug. "I didn't really know her, only met her when she came to the museum."

"Do you know why she came to the museum?"

"The same as everyone, I suppose, to see where Hemingway lived and wrote. To see the Hemingway cats. She seemed really interested in the cats."

"Do you work here?"

"Yes," he smiled and held out his hand. "I'm Robert Truman." He gave a little laugh. "No relationship to Harry Truman. People always ask me that. Well, people who come to the museum, that is. Because of the Truman White House, you know." He shrugged again.

Ginger realized that Robert Truman was nervous because he was painfully shy despite his good looks.

"What do you do here, Mr. Truman?"

"Oh, call me Robert. Everyone does." He cleared his throat. "I'm actually doing graduate work on Hemingway and this summer I'm interning as a guide. It helps to get the flavor of the place he loved so much."

"Yes, I suppose it does." Ginger wasn't sure how to elicit the information she needed so she simply asked him straight out. "Why did you come to the Paradise looking for Liberty?"

He blushed. "She seemed to like me," he said. "I thought I'd ask her to dinner. Or maybe just a drink."

"I see."

He cleared his throat. "I'm not good at that sort of thing. Asking women out, that is. I thought I could stop in the Paradise and if I saw her then... Well, I don't know what then."

"You hadn't seen her the night before?"

"No. She was at the museum during the day. The idea of the cats having movie star names fascinated her. She said she liked the idea of trying on the name of a Hollywood icon.

Marilyn Monroe was her preference although she liked Lauren Bacall, too."

"I'm sorry about your friend," Ginger said.

He nodded. Then his gaze fell on the folder she held. "Can I help you with something?" he asked.

"No," Ginger said, "I was just making some notes for myself about the titles of the books in here. I think I'll try to improve myself by reading some of them."

"An admirable goal. If there's anything I can do to help, suggestions or that sort of thing, I'm happy to do so."

"Thanks, Robert. And stop by the Paradise anytime. I serve tea from three until five thirty. I'll let you try some of my key lime pie."

SAWYER COULDN'T BE INDUCED to reveal any more information about his business with Annette but Trout didn't really need for him to do so. The nature of the object he was pursuing had been established regardless of what the actual prize might be.

He left the marina office and turned to retrace his steps back to the Paradise. Out of the corner of his eye he caught a glimpse of a silhouette. Someone had been standing among the roots of a banyan tree and when Trout passed by on the other side of the street, that someone moved. It was the way he moved that triggered the memory of the intruder for Trout.

The moment Trout turned and zeroed in on the slender figure, he broke and ran, proof positive that whoever he was, he had been either tailing Trout or spying on Sawyer. This time Trout had the advantage. This part of Key West was Trout's home base. The intruder wouldn't lose him again.

Trout anticipated the right turn onto Love Lane. The

smaller streets offered better opportunity for his culprit to slip through residential areas and disappear. A car backed from an almost hidden driveway into the runner's path and blocked him. This caused the runner to check his pace and gave Trout the small advantage he needed. Just as his target was about to outmaneuver him once again, Trout reached out and caught the back of his shirt. Quick he might be, but he was no match for Trout's strength. Trout held tight to the dark blue tee shirt as his prisoner squirmed and kicked.

In the scuffle, the runner's baseball cap fell off. "Stop it!" Trout said. "You're caught."

The face that turned to him in fear wasn't a man after all, but a woman. Actually, it was a young girl, not much older than her mid-teens. The revelation caught Trout off guard and for a split second he was speechless.

"Who are you?" he finally asked but he needed no reply to his question. The sweet aroma of tobacco permeated the air around them. This, then, was the menace who had wreaked so much havoc on the staff at the Paradise.

When she remained silent he gathered the collar of her shirt more securely and marched her in the direction of the Paradise.

With his free hand he fished his cell phone out of his pocket and called Ginger.

"Get in touch with Duncan," he told her. "Have him swing by the business of Geraldo Mechoso." His captive tried to break free at those words. "It's a cigar factory unless I'm very much mistaken. He should be able to figure out where. Have him bring Mechoso to the bed and breakfast. It's time we got some answers."

CHAPTER ELEVEN

I admit to being caught off guard by the apprehension of our young prowler. She doesn't seem very villainous to me but then looks can be deceiving.

Duncan and a very unhappy Geraldo Mechoso sit across the room from Trout and his prize catch. Ginger is pouring tea that is being ignored. Who can blame them. We're finally going to get to the heart of this matter.

Duncan clears his throat. "Who wants to start?"

When no one responds he says, "I don't have all day. We can always do this down at the station."

"What have you done, Evita?" Mechoso asks.

She makes no reply.

"I'll tell you what she's done," Trout says. "She sent two people to the hospital with major head injuries and poisoned a third."

"Evita! Tell me this isn't true." Mechoso abruptly rose to his feet, his expression one of grief and disbelief.

Duncan stands as well, ready to act as necessary.

"I didn't kill anyone," the young woman called Evita says. "I swear

it. I was there but I didn't do anything to her." Tears begin to trail down her face. "Please, Papa, you have to believe me."

"I'm the one you have to convince," Duncan says. "Tell me what happened. Otherwise, I have no choice but to charge you with murder."

"Murder!" Mechoso and Evita cry in unison.

Duncan allows the silence to lengthen until Evita drops her head and says, "I didn't do anything to her. I was in the bathroom. I hid behind the door when I heard the key turning in the lock."

I leap onto Evita's lap and her hands automatically begin to furrow through my sleek black coat.

"Who was with her," Duncan asks. "Did you see him?"

Evita looks bewildered and shakes her head. "No one. She was alone."

Trout follows my lead and asks, "What happened, Evita," in that quiet tone of his that draws people to confide in him.

She looks at Trout, fear evident in every aspect of her being. "I don't know. The door opened and I could hear her fumbling at the lock, trying to fit the key on the inside of it. I realized I'd been caught."

"How did you do it without her creating a fuss?" Duncan asks.

"I didn't do anything!" Evita wails. "She was drunk, okay? Stumbling across the room. I could hear her. She went over to the window and closed it. I was panicking, trying to decide how I was going to get out of there."

"How did you get out?" Ginger asks.

Evita looked from Duncan to Ginger and finally her gaze came to rest on her father. "I heard her drop something, then she coughed a couple of times." She swallows and holds me to her chest. "The room got very quiet. I waited. After a while, I couldn't stand it any longer so I slipped from behind the door." She looks up at Duncan. "She was passed out on the bed."

"No one else was in the room?" he asks.

Evita shakes her head.

"*What then,*" *Trout wants to know.*

"*I left.*"

"*How?*" *Duncan, Trout, and Ginger ask in unison.*

"*Through the second window.*"

All three of them look from one to the other. Duncan takes Evita by the arm and when she stands, I'm dumped onto the floor. He marches her out into the foyer and up the stairs. When we reach the Toucan Suite, Ginger unlocks the door.

"*Show me,*" *Duncan says.*

Evita looks at everyone crowded into the room. She crosses to the other side, slips behind the wing back chair sitting in front of the second window, and draws back the drapes. She then lowers the top panel of it. With her hands on the top of the lower panel, she lifts her body over and out, and looks back into the room at Duncan, Trout, Ginger, and Geraldo Mechoso. "Like that," she says.

Trout is the first to reach the window and examine it. "*The sash is cut. It appears to be locked but without the tension of the pulley weights, it can't be secured.*"

Ginger examines the damage to the window mechanism. "*This is an old cut. Why didn't I realize this before now?*"

"*Probably because this window isn't used. The chair placement creates a natural traffic pattern from the room onto the gallery through the other window. It could have been this way for years.*"

"*How did you know you could get in and out this way?*" *Duncan asks Evita as he opens the other window and steps out onto the gallery.*

"*I didn't.*" *She gives a little shake of her head and a slight shrug.* "*I thought I'd go through this window so that when she woke up she wouldn't realize anyone had been in the room. The chair blocks it and who bothers to move a chair and check the lock?*" *She looks from one to the other.* "*Nobody.*"

"*That still doesn't explain how you got into the room in the first place,*" *Duncan says.*

"Oh, that part was easy. No one was around so I used the entry card, got the key off the board, went upstairs and unlocked the door."

"How did you get an entry card?" Ginger wants to know.

"I stole it from the desk earlier in the day."

This doesn't make Ginger happy. In fact, she's looking rather dismayed. Trout moves to her side and places an arm around her shoulders. She's feeling guilty, I expect, about the lack of security that has allowed these events to unfold at the Paradise. Well, there's nothing for it but to learn from our mistakes. In time she'll realize that Liberty's death would have occurred regardless of her security measures.

Trout is staring out across the gallery, lost in thought, it would seem. "How did Liberty get into her room when she arrived?"

"I left the key in the lock. I was going..." Evita looked at her father. "I was going to be in and out in a hurry but I couldn't find it. That's how she caught me off guard."

"So you thought that since she was drunk she wouldn't remember the key in the door when she woke the next morning."

"Exactly. That's why I needed the room to be locked from the inside."

"How did you get off the gallery?" Ginger asked.

Geraldo Mechoso answers for her. "She's a world class gymnast." The look of disappointment on his face is heartbreaking.

"Out and over the railing," Duncan says with a sigh and a shake of his head.

"That means Liberty really did die of a dose of GHB that occurred at some point before she returned to the Paradise," Ginger says.

Duncan rolls his shoulders in a shrug. "The obvious answer is usually the right answer."

Yes. Our man Duncan is correct on this one. Maybe the laid back attitude masks a deep one. An air of regret that hovers around him tells me he's 'in the picture', as they say, on the current status of Ginger and Trout's relationship as well. No, not a bad detective after all.

. . .

GINGER HANDED the old notebook page across the kitchen work table to Duncan. He read it, turned it over and checked the back, then handed it to Trout.

"So?"

"That's what everyone is looking for."

"An old sheet of paper with a bunch of scribbling and scratch outs on it?"

"It's Hemingway's scribbling." Ginger took the bottle of tequila from the pantry and set up three shot glasses. "That's what it's supposed to be anyway." She sliced a lime.

"How do you know this?" Trout asked.

She looked over his shoulder at the page and pointed at the notation in the bottom left hand corner. "*Ask Chink* and the question mark."

"Who's Chink?" Duncan wanted to know.

"Eric Dorman-Smith, nicknamed Chink. He was an Irishman in the British Expeditionary Force and a patient at a hospital in Milan where Hemingway was recuperating during World War One." She passed around the shots and lime. "They became friends."

"Why does this matter?" Trout asked.

"Hemingway's character is Catherine, see there?" she pointed. "She's modeled after Agnes von Kurowsky, Hemingway's first love and his nurse while he was recuperating."

"I don't see that this means anything."

"I did some research on Hemingway while you were gone to see Sawyer. Catherine is the main character in *A Farewell to Arms.* He used people from his life as the basis of many of his characters throughout his career. I think this sheet of paper is meant to represent an early draft of that manuscript or at least notes he was making in the early stages of the idea for the story. The *Ask Chink* notation could be a note to himself to verify something, a memory or fact from that time."

"But there's really nothing here," Trout said.

"It isn't so much about what's here as to when it was written. When Hemingway and his first wife, Hadley, were first living in Paris in the early nineteen twenties, he was in Switzerland covering the Lausanne Peace Conference. Hadley was supposed to bring all his manuscripts from Paris so he could show them to an editor named Steffens who was also covering the conference. She packed up everything he had written in a suitcase that was stolen from the train before it even left the *Gare de Lyon* station. And it was *everything* Hemingway had written."

"Was it the manuscript of *A Farewell to Arms?*" Duncan asked.

"That's just it," Ginger said. "No one knows. It's thought that it was mainly early short stories and poetry but possibly the beginnings of other works. He wasn't published at that time except for his journalism. All his great achievements came afterward."

"You think someone found his stolen suitcase full of his earliest work." Trout said.

"I think that might be what Annette is trying to make Sawyer and Fortesque believe."

"What makes you think it's this early stolen work?"

"The reference to Chink, for one thing. The war years and their friendship would still be fresh in his mind in 1922. It's reasonable to assume he would be forming ideas for the story at that time. But mainly because that's the only thing that fits."

Duncan rolled his shoulders, rubbed the crease in his forehead, and sighed. "Explain to me why this fits more than any other hare-brained idea."

"The theft occurred in Paris. It's assumed the thief realized there was nothing of value in the suitcase and threw the contents away. Or maybe he didn't. Maybe he hid it in his attic in the Latin quarter or some other tenement and someone has only just discovered it."

"Maybe you've been watching too much Father Brown or Grantchester." Duncan replied. "If no one has found Hemingway's stolen papers in all this time, they're not going to be found. This is all a crock."

"Maybe," Ginger said. "But it's plausible enough to make a good scam."

"Where did you find this?" Trout asked.

"I picked it up from the floor under Annette's bed when we were cleaning the room. At the time I thought it was trash so I threw it in the bin. Later, after you left, it suddenly dawned on me what it was. It was the notation about Chink that made me realize it."

"Could this be the real thing?" Duncan asked.

The three of them exchanged a look.

No one said anything into the silence then they all reached for their glasses, threw back their shots, and bit into the lime wedges.

"WHAT WILL HAPPEN TO EVITA, DUNCAN?" Trout asked.

"They'll book her on the charges of breaking and entering and assault. That will hold her until Mechoso posts bail, if the judge allows it."

"You mean she's going to jail?" Ginger asked.

Duncan spread his hands in exasperation. "What do you think happens to criminals, Ginger?"

"She's just a kid." Trout said.

"A kid who sent two people to the hospital and one to the morgue."

"You don't believe that," Trout said.

"Yeah, well it gives me leverage until she comes clean about why she was in that room. We won't know she's truly innocent of poisoning Liberty until we know if she was looking for this sheet of paper. Why would anyone think Liberty had it in the first place?"

"Because Evita thought Liberty was Annette Benoit." Trout said. "Somehow Evita learned about a literary agent coming to town to auction a lost Hemingway manuscript to the highest bidder. She knew that it was a blond woman and that the Toucan Suite had been reserved for her."

"How did you know about the room reservations?" Ginger asked.

"It's the only thing that makes sense. You said Liberty didn't want the Bird Cage. That tells me you had to have had that room on the books for her when she arrived, right?"

"Yes."

"Instead she ends up in the suite you planned to put your foreign guest in, the one with the added amenity of more space and access to the gallery."

"Right," Ginger said. "But how would Evita know?"

"Is your computer system password protected?" Trout asked.

"Yes."

"Does the staff know what the password is?"

Ginger hesitated. "Yes."

"And would the password be *bird of paradise?*"

Ginger's face turned red. "All this is my fault."

"No it isn't," Duncan said. "Liberty was drugged off the premises. That could have happened regardless of where she was staying. This isn't about you and the Paradise, it's about someone willing to kill for scribblings on a piece of paper."

"What I don't understand is how Evita knew about any of this. It's true Geraldo came to the bed and breakfast looking for Annette before her disappearance with a story line that they had an appointment. He seemed truly caught off guard when he discovered what Evita had been doing. Regardless, he's involved somehow." Trout said.

He stared out the kitchen window at the two Hemingway cats making their way across the lawn. "You should talk to Sawyer." He said to Duncan. "He knows more about this than he's willing to tell me. Maybe he'll feel more inclined to answer your questions."

THE THOUGHT *of young Evita languishing in jail has me feeling rather melancholy. It doesn't sit well with Trout either. Such an outcome must take him back to memories of his former life.*

Oh, dear, I do believe I'm depressing myself. I think what I need is a cool, quiet spot to reflect on the happenings at the Paradise and let the little gray cells, as Poirot, would say, do what they do.

I find the climb to the fire escape landing is well worth the effort. A nice breeze rustles the palm fronds and creates a delightful background noise against the intrusion of the life of the city. I understand why it's a favorite spot of Megs and Bartholomew. Up here you're removed from the daily drama.

As I sprawl in the shade of the bed and breakfast I feel as if I'm adrift on the high seas, the shushing of the palm fronds nudging me to the edge of sleep. Perhaps just a little snooze, then. It was probably such a somnolent state as this that Megs dreamed up the notion of Annette being a spy and hiding things.

I sigh. That ease is suddenly gone. What is it about Megs' imaginings that has left me awake and alert? That it was a shared dream, of course. She and Bartholomew both said they saw her hiding things, red and black things. Not too large things and not too small things.

I scramble to me feet and look into the window. Where could they witness something being hidden? There is only the view of the long hallway. A door near the other end opens into the Bird Cage. Next to that is the door to... Oh what silly name does Ginger call that guest room? The Blue Heron, that's it. Last is the door to the linen closet, right here, just inside the window.

GINGER LOOKED up from sifting flour into a bowl when Trouble came dashing through the back door and slid to a stop at her feet.

"Yeow!"

"Not now, Trouble, I have my hands full."

"Yeow! Yeow!"

He trotted to the doorway that led from the kitchen into the dining room. When Ginger didn't stop what she was doing and follow after him, he came back, stood on his hind legs, and caught her apron with his claws.

"Seriously?" Ginger dusted the flour from her hands and disengaged his claws. "What is the matter with you?"

He twined between her legs, complaining all the while.

Ginger sighed, removed her apron, and followed after him. He was already at the top of the stairs before she could get to the foyer.

Trout looked up from the brochures he was organizing on

an entry way table when Ginger strode across the foyer. "Where's the fire?"

"Apparently it's upstairs."

Trout fell in behind Ginger and they followed Trouble up the stairs, around the landing and to the back hallway. When they turned the corner, he was sitting in front of the linen closet.

"Oh, for pity's sake," Ginger said. "I think he's gone completely bonkers. This obsession with closed doors is going to be the death of me."

"Yeow!" Trouble stretched up and clawed at the door knob of the linen closet.

"You're not getting in there and get cat hair all over my clean linens," Ginger said as she marched down the hallway and caught Trouble up in her arms. "I have enough work to do without having to rewash all the sheets and towels."

Trouble squirmed from her grasp and began clawing in earnest at the door.

"He seems to be after something," Trout said.

"If you're implying I have mice, I'm going to knock your lights out, Trout." She tried to capture Trouble but he evaded her grasp. "That's the last thing I need with a house full of guests arriving the day after tomorrow."

Trout reached past her and opened the door to the linen closet.

"Trout!" Ginger wailed.

Trouble dashed into the enclosure and began pawing among the stacks of sheets and towels.

"Great," Ginger muttered."

"Sorry, Ginger," Trout said, "but I think there's something more going on here than him being contrary and obsessed with closed doors." Trout began taking the sheets out of the closet and stacking them on the floor of the hallway.

When he lifted a stack of towels from the third shelf from the bottom of the closet, a black leather case trimmed in red fell to the floor.

"What in the heck," Ginger said as she picked it up.

Trouble sat back on his haunches and said, "Yeow."

"This is what he wanted us to find," Trout said.

"But how..."

Trout looked at the cat, shook his head, and turned to Ginger. "Don't even go there."

THE CASE SAT in the middle of the kitchen work table. Trout and Ginger stared at it. They had tried to open it but it was locked. After a while Ginger said, "We should call Duncan."

"In a bit," Trout said.

"You think this is what everyone is looking for, don't you?"

"Unless the Paradise has become the exchange point for political espionage. Have you had any James Bond look-alikes stay here lately?"

"You should write a book."

"Ha, ha."

"So what should we do?" Ginger asked.

"I think it's time we made everyone show their hands."

"What do you mean?"

"We should round up all the usual suspects and see what they have to say about the mysterious locked case."

"Duncan won't like it."

"Probably not."

"It could be dangerous."

"Yes. It could."

They stared at the case. "Okay," Ginger said.

"Okay?"

"Yeah, okay." She took out her cell phone. "I'll look up Mr. Mechoso's number. Then I'll call the Curry Mansion Inn for Mr. Fortesque. You get Sawyer here."

"Four o'clock?"

Ginger nodded. "Four o'clock."

CHAPTER TWELVE

*W*ell done, Trout. There's no need to let Duncan in on *our little find just yet. Trout's idea to rattle the cage of all the contenders is what we need to find out what's really at stake here. I'm impressed that Ginger is willing to go along with the ploy.*

The two of them might turn out to be decent detectives after all. That overriding desire to crack the case is like catnip. Or whatever bipeds crave. In this case I think it might be tequila. Nasty stuff if you ask me. How anyone could willingly drink something with a worm embalmed in it I'll never know. As they say, to each his own.

What's this? I do believe the thrill of the chase has made Ginger a bit frisky. Enough of that, we still have a mystery to solve.

AT A QUARTER to four Ginger was anxiously watching for the first arrivals. Instead of one of the threesome she was expecting, however, a dark, unmarked sedan pulled into the parking bay of the Paradise. She groaned inwardly. Duncan was about to spoil everything.

Instead of heading directly to the front steps of the bed

and breakfast, he turned and opened the back door of the unmarked police car. Ray Talent emerged, followed by Crissy.

"Trout," Ginger called, "we have company."

Trout appeared from the hallway and when he saw Duncan marching the Talents up the steps of the Paradise, he swore under his breath.

"We'll have to tell him."

"I guess we will."

"Ginger," Duncan said as he entered the foyer.

"Looks like you've been busy," she said.

Duncan rolled his shoulders. "It occurred to me that I don't really have anything to charge these two with, unless, of course, they confess to breaking and entering. But, wait. They can't be charged with B and E if they're paying guests. That and the fact that we don't know for sure that they actually did anything wrong."

Duncan looked hot and tired. Ginger realized the last few days had been a trial for him just as much as it had for her. His pride was also a little dented.

"I'm glad you came, Duncan," Ginger said and licked her lips. "The thing is, Trout and I found this case..."

The Talents looked at each other then back at Ginger.

Duncan looked like he would bite.

"I think it's what everyone is searching for." Ginger glanced from Ray to Crissy Talent. "But we wanted to be sure."

Duncan turned his glare on Trout. "Let me guess," he said. "You didn't call it in because you wanted to open it first. You wanted to make sure it was *significant* to the case." He heaved a soul deep sigh. "The fact that there is no case being beside the point."

"Annette is still missing." Trout said.

"I spoke with Ms. Benoit's assistant. He isn't concerned about her whereabouts."

"Did he tell you why she was in Key West?"

"Business and a little pleasure was his answer to that question. When I inquired if he had heard from her, he said now and then but couldn't say that he'd spoken to her within the last forty-eight hours."

"And that doesn't bother him?"

"No."

"It would bother me," Ginger said.

"Well, you're not French, are you? Apparently, her assistant has better things to do than be bothered with a nuisance visit from *l'officier de police*. It seems that in the absence of his employer, he doesn't feel the need to answer the phone so when they came pounding on his door he flushed all the good stuff."

"Really?"

Duncan threw up his hands in exasperation. "I don't know, Ginger! All I can tell you is that a visit from the police pissed him off and he's not in the least bit worried about Annette."

"Sorry, Duncan."

"Well, I had to call regardless. Key West doesn't need an international incident involving a tourist." He held his finger in the air, closed his eyes, and when he opened them said, "It's been a long day. So tell me about this case you found. Where was it?"

Trout glanced from Ray to Crissy and said, "Maybe we should hear what the Talents have to say about their involvement with Liberty Anderson."

Duncan angled his head in acquiescence and gestured toward the sitting room. Everyone trooped in and sat down except for Duncan. "Ask away," he said.

"Why were you following Ms. Anderson?" Ginger asked.

Ray and Crissy exchanged looks then he cleared his throat. "We didn't do anything wrong, okay? Mr. Fortesque just wanted us to follow her, see who she made contact with, let him know if...if anything changed hands with such contacts."

"By anything you mean..." Trout asked.

Ray shrugged. "Anything."

"Did you search her room?" Ginger asked.

Another quick glance at his wife, then he said, "No. That would be illegal."

Crissy sat forward and said in a nasal twang that reminded Ginger why they used Nashville as their address, "She was supposed to be the other one. The other blond. But we didn't know that." She glanced at her husband. "She was supposed to be in the room next to us. The other one, that is. With the accent." She paused then used her index finger to point for emphasis, "But we didn't know she talked like that. How could we?"

"You didn't take anything from Ms. Anderson's room?" Duncan asked.

The Talents shook their heads.

"Did you ever enter the room?"

They looked at each other then shook their heads again.

"Did you see anyone else enter Ms. Anderson's room?"

Again, the negative shake of the head.

"Why didn't you come back to the Paradise Saturday night?"

Ray said, "Mr. Fortesque paid us and said the job was done."

Duncan looked from Ginger to Trout, his eyebrows raised. "Any more questions?"

"No." Ginger said.

Trout shook his head.

"Get lost," Duncan said to the Talents.

"How are we supposed to get home?" Ray asked.

"Take a taxi with all that money the fat man paid you." Duncan barked.

THE TALENTS just reached the sidewalk on Petronia in front of the Paradise Bed and Breakfast when Mr. Mechoso disembarked from a taxi. He gave them a glance in passing and came on up the walk way.

"He bailed his daughter just a while ago so you can quit worrying on that score," Duncan said.

"Did you learn anything more from her at the station?" Trout asked.

"Not really. I can't figure out how she knew about it, whatever *it* really is, and why she would try to steal it."

"Sawyer told me something interesting about her grandfather."

"That he was buddy buddy with Hemingway? Everyone knows that. I doubt there's an ounce of truth to it except both Ernesto and Hemingway were in Cuba at the same time. The old man used to hang out at Sloppy Joe's telling his tall tales. After a time, no one really listened anymore."

When Mechoso walked through the front door into the foyer he hesitated at the sight of Duncan.

"Don't worry, Mr. Mechoso," Duncan said, "I'm just here for the show."

Ginger came walking in from the dining room carrying the black leather case with red trimming.

"That's it, huh?" Duncan said.

"Do you recognize this, Mr. Mechoso," Trout asked.

He shook his head. "No. Should I?"

"This belongs to Annette Benoit, we believe."

"I see," he replied. "Have you looked inside?"

"Not yet," Ginger said. "We thought it would be better if we waited until all the interested parties were present."

"Who are all the parties?" he asked as the door behind him opened and everyone turned to see Sawyer enter the foyer.

"Geraldo," Sawyer said.

"Sawyer," Mechoso greeted him in return.

"I didn't know you were involved in this."

Mechoso said, "I'm not sure what *this* is."

Sawyer chuckled. "None of us are."

"Why did you come looking for Ms. Benoit, Mr. Mechoso," Trout asked.

"She called me several weeks ago. She was looking for my grandfather. When I told her he died five years ago, she asked if I still had the Hemingway letters."

"And?" Duncan asked.

"I told her yes, those and a photograph of Papa Hemingway with Bumby on a wooden horse my grandfather had made for him. It was a letter of thanks for the gift to the boy. The picture was taken in the garden at *Finca Vigia* in Cuba." He pronounced the word coo-ba, as native Cubans do.

"What was her interest in them?" Ginger wanted to know.

"She said she thought she had a sample of his writing. Hemingway's writing. She wanted to compare it to something from that time in his life to be sure. She also wanted to hear my grandfather's stories."

"There was no offer to buy your letters?"

Mechoso shook his head. "No. She said she'd like to visit with me when she came to Key West. She was doing research on Hemingway and thought my grandfather's stories would give her more insight into her project. She said that she would be staying at the Paradise. There was a message on the telephone two days before I came here. She wanted to set an appointment but when I returned her call, she never answered. I left a message but when I didn't hear from her I decided she had changed her mind."

"You called the Paradise?" Ginger asked.

He shook his head. "No, I called a cell phone number she gave me when we first spoke."

"Why did you come to the Paradise then?" Trout asked.

"I wanted to see the paper. I wanted to see the handwriting and know that it looked like my grandfather's letters."

"Validation of your grandfather's stories," Trout said.

Mechoso made no reply.

"The phone message, that's how Evita knew about Annette and why she was here, isn't it," Trout asked.

Mechoso glanced at Duncan but remained silent.

"She wanted the same thing. To honor her great-grandfather and make people realize he was a truthful man. If the handwriting matched, it would prove to the world that he had known the great Hemingway. That they had been friends." Trout spoke in that voice that reached through the pain and self-doubt.

Mechoso turned away and moved to the bay window in the sitting room. He stood there with his back to them all and stared out into the afternoon shadows.

Into the silence stepped Heronimous Fortesque, slightly breathless from the exertion of climbing the porch steps. His gaze flicked over the black and red case Ginger held in her hands. He smiled all around, his attention lingering on Duncan for a second longer than the rest.

"My, my, what have we here?" He asked.

"These are your fellow treasure hunters, Mr. Fortesque," Trout said, "and this, we believe is the treasure." He nodded toward the case. "Shall we move into the sitting room since everyone is here."

"And where is Ms. Benoit?" He asked as he settled himself on the love seat.

"Not here at present." Trout said.

"Will she be joining us?"

"We hope so, but right now we're interested in what happened to Liberty Anderson."

"That again?" Fortesque said. "I told you she wasn't involved in the matter. The bumbling duo did follow her for a couple of days at my behest before they realized they had the wrong woman."

"Why would you hire someone to follow Ms. Benoit?" Duncan asked.

"Who're you?" Fortesque wanted to know.

"Detective Moore, Key West Police, currently looking into the circumstances surrounding Mrs. Anderson's death and Ms. Benoit's disappearance."

"Ms. Benoit is missing? What about the Hemingway papers? How can we conduct business if she's missing?"

"Your concern is touching," Duncan said.

"So this is a gathering of the *usual suspects*, is it?" Fortesque laughed. "You, Detective Moore are no Louis Renault, and you," he inclined his head toward Trout, "are certainly no Humphrey Bogart." With a wave of his hand he said, "Please. Proceed. Tell us what any of us has to gain by Ms. Anderson's death or Ms. Benoit's disappearance."

Ginger leaned in close to Trout and said in a low voice. "It worked so much better in the movies."

Sawyer spoke up. "Can we at least see what's in the case?

Fortesque is right. No one here had any reason to harm either of those women. We all very much want Ms. Benoit to be alive and well and ready to pull a rabbit out of the hat."

Ginger placed the case on the coffee table. "It's locked," she said, "and we don't have the combination."

Sawyer slapped his hand against his forehead, Fortesque groaned and sat back on the love seat, Mechoso came to stand over the case. After a few seconds he asked, "Did you try Hemingway's birthday? It's a four digit lock. Start with the year, eighteen ninety-nine."

Ginger knelt beside the coffee table and tried the numbers. She looked up at Mechoso and shook her head.

"July 21st doesn't lend itself to the number of digits. Maybe zero seven two one."

Those numbers didn't work either.

"This is probably a case she's had for years and the code could be any number significant to her life. This is a gross waste of time." Duncan said. "We'll never figure out the combination."

"And why would you?" asked a heavily accented woman's voice.

Everyone turned to see Annette Benoit standing in the entry into the sitting room with Jerry, the bartender from the Green Parrot, at her side. She was wearing an oversized man's tee shirt with a man's belt wrapped twice around her waist. She was very much alive and she looked fabulous.

WELL, now, this is a sleight of hand I hadn't foreseen. Where, I wonder, has the lovely Annette been for the past two days? Pray one of these men can lift their chins off the floor to ask.

Duncan is the first to recover. A ladies' man usually is nimble with his reactions.

"Ms. Benoit," he says with a certain something in his voice, "I'm Duncan Moore with the Key West Police and we've been concerned about you."

"I remember you," she says.

"Well, it wasn't under the best of circumstances. That's why Ginger contacted me when you didn't return to your room for two nights."

"Why should I?" she asks. "This house is not safe. At every turn people are being knocked in the head or dead. A man was in my room." *She is warming to the injustice of it all.* "In my locked room."

"We've caught the trespasser," Moore says.

"Oh." *His comment takes some of the wind out of her sails.* "Well, still, I couldn't think about sleeping here after what happened."

"Where have you been," Ginger asks.

I glance at Jerry, the bartender from the Green Parrot and know the answer. Ginger is sweet and for someone who has seen a lot of life, a little naïve.

The straightforwardness of the Aussies comes out in full when Jerry says, "She's been staying with me."

Never mind chivalry, then. But at least my suspicions are confirmed.

"It would have been nice to know," Ginger says with a touch of frost in her voice.

Annette turns to Ginger with a look that beautiful women reserve for all other women. "I did not think of it. Why would you worry about me?"

Why, indeed? Or maybe it's just that she's French.

Never mind all that, it's time we got to the contents of the case. This has been at the heart of all the turmoil at the Paradise and I, for one, won't rest until I know what has caused all this grief for Ginger.

Trout appears to be in agreement with me.

"This is your case, Ms. Benoit?" he asks.

She flicks her head, sending her blond curls swinging back from her face. "Yes. This is my case. You had no right to try to open it."

"It's abandoned property," Ginger says. "It wasn't in your room. There's no identification on it. How could I begin to guess at ownership?"

Score one for Ginger. That red hair isn't wasted on her.

Annette once again focuses her attention on Ginger. You can see that she realizes she has misjudged the proprietress of the Paradise. She draws herself up to a new level of haughtiness and says, "I know the combination to the lock."

"Prove it," Trout says.

Annette lets her gaze travel around the room full of people. "Why should I? I don't know who these people are. The contents are very valuable and private."

"Is that why you hid them in the linen closet?" Ginger asks. "A very public place where all the staff of the Paradise might find them?"

"It was to be only for a day or two," Annette says. "The rooms were all empty except for the couple on the front. I didn't see the staff needing enough fresh towels to get to the level where the case was hidden." She looks to Duncan in appeal. "I knew someone was searching for it. That's why that man was in my room."

Apparently Duncan has gotten a handle on himself. He says, "You still have to prove it's your case. The only way I know you can do that is to open it."

Annette is silent. I can almost see the wheels turning. How to get what she wants without giving anything.

Finally she says, "Introduce me to all these men."

H. Fortesque steps forward, takes her hand, places a kiss on the back of it, and smiles. "Surely you remember me, Ms. Benoit."

She returns his smile. "Of course, Mr. Fortesque."

Mechoso nods his head, almost a bow. "I'm Geraldo Mechoso. We spoke on the phone about my father's letters."

"Yes," Annette says, "so kind you were to take my call."

That left Sawyer. He stands back from the others, biding his time. The mark of a man accustomed to getting his way though you would not think it from his appearance. He's playing the long game.

Annette comes to him. She extends her hand and he takes it but doesn't follow Fortesque's example. He merely holds it.

"Mr. Sawyer Daniels, I presume," she says.

"Ms. Benoit."

Annette steps back and lets her gaze travel over all the them before settling on Duncan. "I will open it, but only with a select few present." She angles her head toward Duncan. "You, of course, as a representative of the local authority. But only to see that I know the combination and the case is truly my possession."

"And?" Duncan asks.

"Mr. Fortesque and Mr. Daniels." She pauses, "And Mr. Mechoso."

Duncan glances to Ginger then Trout. He nods his head to Annette. "Deal."

Ginger starts to protest and he says, "You want to get to the end of this or not?"

With a sigh, Ginger crosses her arms and acquiesces.

Duncan herds everyone out of the sitting room except the precious few Annette has designated. And, of course, moi. He closes the double doors.

JERRY LOOKED from Ginger to Trout and said, "What's this all about?"

"It's a long story, Jerry." Trout could feel Ginger's annoyance. He wasn't real pleased himself at being booted from the great reveal.

"Well," Jerry said, "it was a good time while it lasted. I'd best be moving on. I'm on the clock at five."

"Right," Trout said.

Ginger seemed to rouse from her funk. "Jerry, thanks. For spreading the word about the Paradise."

"You bet." He turned toward the front door and stopped. "You know that woman you were asking about? The dead one?"

Trout perked up. "Yeah?"

"I could have sworn I saw her on the way over here today. Well, an older version of her, anyway."

"Mel." Trout and Ginger said in unison.

"Yeah, well, it kind of gave me that feeling, you know? Like someone walking on your grave."

"She's not a ghost, Jerry," Trout said. "She'll move on as soon as she cuts through the red tape about her husband's ashes."

"That's supposed to reassure me?" Jerry asked.

Both Trout and Ginger laughed.

"It sounds spookier than it is, really."

"If you say so. Anyway, catch you later." With that Jerry crossed the foyer and out the door just as Duncan appeared from the sitting room, closing the double doors behind him.

"So?" Ginger asked.

"It's hers. At least she knew the combination and that's good enough for me."

When he said nothing further, Ginger prompted, "Well?"

"Well, nothing. It has several file folders in it." Before Ginger could ask anything else, he raised his hand to silence her. "She wouldn't take anything out of the case while I was in there. For the eyes of her clientele only, she said."

"Duncan!" Ginger cried.

"Sorry, Ginger. She's within her rights, short of a suspicion of terrorist materials or drugs, to keep her business private."

Trout watched Mechoso through the glass panes of the double doors. He had donned a pair of white gloves and held a yellowed sheet of paper with reverence. Regardless of the authenticity of the papers, Trout felt they had accomplished at least one good thing.

"About Evita," Trout said.

Duncan rolled his shoulders. "It's been a long few days, Trout. Why don't we let that rest until we all have clearer heads. She's out on bail, safe at home with her parents. That's good enough for now."

"You can't charge her, Duncan," Ginger said.

"I already have, Ginger," he replied, a note of aggrievement in his voice.

"She's a young girl. Think what this will do to her life going forward." Ginger hesitated. "Besides, I won't press charges and neither will Jules."

"At this point it isn't up to you."

"I won't testify against her."

Trout touched Ginger's elbow. "Tomorrow, Ginger," he said. "Duncan's right. We all could use a good night's sleep."

Duncan watched the interaction between Trout and Ginger and turned to look out the beveled glass door of the Paradise. "What made you look in the linen closet for the case?"

Trout and Ginger exchanged a glance.

"We were making up the rooms." Trout said. "Clean sheets, towels."

"We found it by accident," Ginger said.

"You on the payroll of the Paradise now?" Duncan asked Trout.

"Just helping out," he said.

"Uh huh." Duncan looked back at Trout and Ginger, a shadow of doubt in his eyes. "Well, if you quit your day job, you might make a half way decent detective."

"Except we never did find out why Liberty was murdered."

"Just an unfortunate coincidence," Duncan said. "A soon-to-be divorcee in paradise looking to have a good time ended up the victim of a would-be rapist. End of story."

"I guess you're right," Trout said as he jangled the change in his pocket.

"I'm closing the books on this one," Duncan said, "and taking a few days of well deserved time off. I don't want to hear another peep about goings on at the Paradise."

"Then you'd be well advised to let Mel have Arty's ashes. She's like a bull terrier and I don't think you'll get any peace until she has them."

"What are you talking about?" Duncan asked.

"The ashes. From the Toucan suite. You know, Liberty Anderson's box of her dead husband's ashes."

"The other wife." Duncan said.

"The ex-wife," Ginger corrected him.

"She already has them," Duncan said.

"Since when?" Trout asked.

"Since, I don't know, the night she hit town."

Trout and Ginger looked at each other.

"Something isn't right," Ginger said to Trout as they watched Duncan walk down the steps of the Paradise and get into his car.

"And I think I know what it is," Trout said.

Ginger looked at him. "Why is she still in town?"

"Exactly," Trout said. "Especially since she's made such a stink about the cost of staying in Key West."

They turned in unison toward the stairs and hurried to the top of the landing. In the open doorway of the Toucan Suite they let their gazes travel around the room. What was it that kept Melissa Anderson in town long after there was any need? What was it she sought? Ginger thought she knew. The only question was, where would Liberty have hidden it?

"The safe," Ginger said.

Trout opened the armoire to find the door of the safe standing open. "Too obvious. Let's start with the bed," he said.

They stripped the four poster bed of the linens, checking thoroughly within the folds as they went. There was nothing under the mattress and Ginger shimmied under the bed to get a good look at the underside. No luck there.

All the drawers of the dressing table and highboy were removed and checked. Behind the armoire proved to be a dead end.

Hot and tired, Ginger sat back on her heels. "Where would she hide it?" she asked into the silence.

The sound of voices below and the closing of the front door gave notice that the party sequestered in the sitting room had broken up. Trouble came wandering into the room, an inquisitive look on his face.

Ginger scratched between his ears when he came to sit in front of her. "Where is it, huh?" she asked the cat.

He looked up at her and blinked then sat gazing out the tall window.

Trout sat on the edge of the mattress and asked, "Where would you hide something that the average person wouldn't think to look? Something so out of the norm that even the cleaning staff wouldn't be a risk?"

Ginger shrugged. "We've checked beneath all the drawers for an envelope taped underneath. All the furniture, even the rug." She shook her head. "Where else is there? She must have done the same thing Annette did. It has to be hidden somewhere else in the Paradise."

Trout didn't respond and he didn't move. His gaze was fixed on the middle distance, lost in thought.

Trouble jumped onto the shelf in a recess of the room between the front wall and the enclosed duct space for the air conditioner venting. It served as a small work space and in the corner was a coffee pot for guests to have a fresh cup while they prepared for their day. He sniffed at the little basket containing condiments.

Ginger watched him and suddenly inhaled sharply. "The microwave."

Trout stood.

"In the cabinet below the television," she said.

He opened the cabinet, then the door to the microwave. It was empty.

"Well, it was a thought," Ginger said, disappointment in her voice.

"We need to undo all this havoc," Trout said. He adjusted the mattress with a push of his knee and pulled a sheet from the pile of linens they had taken from the bed.

It took them twice as long to restore everything to order as it had for them to wreck it. They stood in the middle of the room and eyed their handiwork. "That was a wild goose chase," Ginger said.

"We could be wrong," Trout said.

They looked at each other and shook their heads.

"Where to look, then," he asked.

"I haven't the foggiest."

"We're done here, I guess," Trout said as he pushed the bathroom door wide and glanced inside. The cat was sitting on the closed toilet seat.

"Yeow."

"I've already checked in here," he said to the cat. "But it was a good thought."

"Are you talking to the cat?" Ginger asked with a smile.

"I suppose I am."

"There's no place to hide anything in the bathroom. We've checked the cabinet beneath the sink and the medicine chest. Let's call this room a wrap." She motioned toward the cat. "Come on Trouble. This room is ready for guests and I don't want to have to revisit it with the vacuum chasing cat hair."

"Yeow." He said and remained where he sat.

Ginger and Trout watched the cat who in turn watched them. She let her gaze travel around the room until it came to rest on the stack of snowy white towels on the shelf above the toilet.

The aha moment was like a chill finger running down her spine. She crossed the bathroom and began shaking out the towels. On the third one in the pile, a blue legal document fell to the tiled floor.

"The will," Ginger and Trout said in unison.

CHAPTER THIRTEEN

I confess to having been fooled by Mel Anderson. I'm a big enough cat to acknowledge that her aggressiveness toward Liberty was the perfect foil to any inquiries about her story. Lesson learned, as my dear old Da would say.

It was a good ploy and it worked for a while but like Trout and Ginger, I don't believe in coincidences. The resolution to the case didn't sit well with me or them and to their credit, they refused to let it go.

For all the skullduggery surrounding Annette Benoit and her found treasure, the true crime was the original one, the murder of Liberty Anderson. The motive was a classic one; money. She as much as told us so when we first met her at the Paradise. Her ex-husband's beneficiary hadn't yet been settled. In the end, it was all about the inheritance of his estate.

I should have adhered to the ages old truism. It's always the ex-wife.

If she hadn't hung around Key West in the hope of gaining access to the Paradise to search for the will, she might have gotten away with it.

Duncan has taken Mel into custody on the circumstantial evidence we now have. It's only a matter of time until all that dogged legwork *that is the bane of policing bears fruit and someone will come forward with further information. Two women who looked so much alike can't have gone unnoticed by some local.*

It's a lucky thing for Duncan that the search of Mel's residence has produced evidence that she "cooked" her own GHB. It will be a simple enough task for the forensics team to prove it's the same batch that was found in Liberty's system.

Mel's computer is in the hands of the police in DC. My guess is they will find that the complaint about the Hemingway cats was generated from her laptop. That was rather a clever touch by Mel, to move the crime scene from a location where suspicion would naturally fall on her.

The guests for the convention arrived yesterday. Mimosas are free flowing and everyone is in a jovial mood except for the crusty old bat in the Blue Heron. I may be in paradise but I wouldn't have Ginger's job for all the tea in China.

Trout is manning the tiki bar and Harry is fetching and carrying. Jules will return to work tomorrow and Ginger is happy. All is well in Paradise.

TROUT WATCHED Duncan stroll across the side lawn of the Paradise to the tiki bar. "Duncan," he said by way of greeting, "you're looking rested."

The detective deposited himself on one of the bar stools. "It's amazing what a couple of nights' sleep will do," he replied. He looked around at the people reclining by the pool, laughing and having a good time. "Looks like it's business as usual."

"Pretty much."

Duncan watched Trout mix a drink and hand it off to Harry. "So, you give up the charter business or what?"

"No," Trout said. "Just helping out until Jules returns tomorrow."

"Huh." Duncan took a sip of the gin and tonic Trout placed before him. "How's Ginger?"

"I think she'll be fine. Still a little squeamish about Liberty dying on the premises but that will pass with time."

"Didn't seem to hurt her business."

"No. Sawyer was right about that. She's been getting a lot of calls for the Toucan Suite. Apparently there are a lot of people who like the idea of a dead body in a locked room."

"How'd that get out, I wonder."

"Beats me but the Ghosts and Gravestones tour is already including it in their spiel like he said they would."

"Where is he anyway," Duncan asked. "Haven't seen him since the great reveal."

Trout grinned. "On the *Big Buddha*. With Ms. Benoit."

Duncan laughed. "You don't say. Looks like they struck a deal. Was the article of interest genuine?"

"Who knows but I think Sawyer will enjoy finding out. After all..."

"She's French," Trout and Duncan said in unison.

GINGER CHECKED on Jules at the front desk, straightened the tourist brochures and wandered out onto the porch. Trout was lounging on the swing reading *Old Possums Book of Particular Cats*. He looked up when Ginger crossed to where he sat.

"Caught out," he said with a smile.

Ginger laughed. "Come on," she reached out her hand to him, "let's walk down to Mallory Pier and watch the sunset."

Trout took her hand and they strolled south to the gathering point of tourists and conchs alike for mother nature's grand finale. Trouble trotted along at their heels.

There was a light breeze off the water and Trout stood

behind Ginger, his arms around her as they faced west and waited. On a piling in front of them Trouble sat, also looking out across the water as the last of the sun turned the sky orange and red in a spectacular halo.

"What do you imagine he's thinking," Trout asked Ginger.

"I believe he's contemplating his singular name," she replied.

ABOUT THE AUTHOR

As a child growing up in the rural South, **Rebecca Barrett** became a lifelong reader and story teller with the arrival of the Bookmobile. That marvelous innovation of the county library system opened the door onto the greater world for her and set her on a path of tall tales that has been a vital part of her life since she was eight.

There were always cats and dogs on the farm. Dogs were easy, but cats, now that was a whole other story. The study of cats gives life to all kinds of personalities and creates a wealth of characters in a child's mind, especially if you're the only girl in a small community rife with rough and tumble boys. So, now, all those hours spent spinning stories around her cats has spurred her imagination to enter the world of Trouble, the Sherlock of black cat detectives.

Trouble in Paradise is Rebecca Barrett's second book in the Familiar Legacy mystery series. She also writes historical women's fiction. *Road's End* is set in the South between the two world wars and is a story of love, betrayal, and dark secrets of three generations of Carroll women ruled by passion. Samples of her short stories and children's stories can be found on her website.

www.rebeccabarrett.com

facebook.com/rebeccabarrett.author

twitter.com/rebeccacbarrett

goodreads.com/RBarrett

amazon.com/author/rebeccabarrett

bookbub.com/authors/rebecca-barrett

TURNING FOR TROUBLE

Trouble Cat Mysteries #7

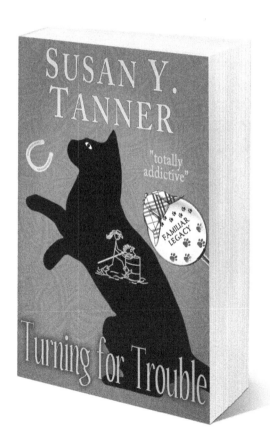

TURNING FOR TROUBLE

Chapter 1

*J*will own up - if I must - to being a bit of a romantic at heart. Ah well, perhaps more than a bit. Even so, never think that small flaw, as some would deem it, in any way undermines my inherent ability to solve any mystery placed in my path. I am, after all, my father's son. My sire, the wondrous Familiar, passed on to me his ability to discern between fact and fiction, to detect truths however skillfully buried amongst untruths. These are no small traits and absolutely essential to my stock-in-trade of master detective.

Though few would argue that the month of June is touted as the premier wedding month, no one could possibly find fault in this flawless October day. And, quite truthfully, I believe I have never seen a bride more lovely than our Ms. Gorgeous, the intrepid Avery Wilson, momentarily to become Avery Hanna. The name has a nice ring to it and I will accept some accolades as to having ensured the likelihood of a happy outcome for the bride and groom. Ah, but that was another day and another story for my memoirs.

Even so, it is good to be at Summer Valley Ranch once more and *without ominous clouds of danger hanging overhead. Good, too, that the sweltering humidity of summer in the south has been swept away on the dry, crisp breezes of earliest autumn. And, now, with the afternoon fading to evening, the fairy lights twinkle to life in the soft twilight.*

And there! The deed is done. The knot is tie. Let the party commence! I shall celebrate in my own way. As the humans twirl around a dancefloor erected for that purpose, I shall indulge in the fact that Ms. Gorgeous has instructed the waiters at every food station to ensure I'm given a sampling – and more if I desire! – of each of their savory offerings.

MALONE SUMMERS WAS MORE than happy for the bride and groom. Though she didn't see the other woman nearly often enough, she and Avery had become good friends through their shared love of horses. Heaven knew Avery deserved this second opportunity at a happy marriage. Malone didn't much believe in second chances where love was concerned but she wished the best for Avery. The bride was definitely radiant, looking half her age and spinning in the arms of her handsome groom as if she were a teen-ager.

Malone planned to slip into the crowd well before the dance floor was opened up to the wedding guests. She had no intention of dancing though she had loved it once, probably still did, truth be told, but it wasn't a thing she indulged in anymore. There were many things she no longer allowed herself. Life's lessons had been hard but she'd learned them well.

Still smiling at the wedding couple's happiness, she turned and walked straight into a broad chest and strong hands that caught her shoulders ever-so-lightly. Her glance registered a swift impression of an expertly tailored suit in the same moment she caught the light scent of aftershave mixed with pure masculinity. But when she looked up into eyes so pale a grey as to be silver when the light caught them just right, her heart dropped in her chest. She would, she had no doubt, remember those eyes for all of her years. And she had long ago accepted the fact.

"Excuse me," she said quickly and quietly, stepping back and out of the light grip of those hands before he recognized her, if he even would.

"You remember me." He spoke the words with cool assurance, a quiet statement of fact, yet without a trace of ego.

She wanted to refute it, desperately, and almost did, but she'd never been any good with a lie. And he'd know the words for the lie they were. That would be more damning than acknowledging the truth. More than twenty years had passed since they'd last been face to face. She'd seen him in rodeo publications, of course. He'd become one of the who's who in the business management end of the industry where she made her living. But she would have recognized him, regardless.

For years he and his cousin had led team roping in their southeastern circuit, but Cade Delaney had gradually transitioned from competition to management of a rival association. And, recently, when he'd stepped up to become a director for the association where she still competed and paid her dues, she'd realized she would no doubt encounter him at some point. But not here, not now. Not unprepared.

Way too many years ago, Cade had been the one to predict her failure at the path she'd chosen. Just as her father had predicted that failure. But Cade and her father, both of them, had only been half right. And that half was Tyge. Tyge, the rough stock rider she'd left home with at seventeen. Tyge, the

rodeo cowboy she'd loved with, lived with, but never married –
to her parents' lasting shame and her own eventual relief. But
as far as rodeo and the sport of barrel racing, they'd been
wrong. She'd *proven* them wrong. She'd made a good life for
herself in spite of her many mistakes and she earned a damned
good living there.

So, in the end, she didn't lie. She simply made a quiet statement of fact, just as he'd done. "Yes, I remember you." Then
she turned and walked away.

CADE WISHED – JUST for a moment - sincerely wished that he
hadn't come to Avery's wedding. Or that Malone had not
come. Malone was a complication he didn't need. Hell, he
hadn't even known that Avery and Malone knew each other.
His world was peaceful. Orderly. His memories of Malone
Summers were anything but that.

He watched her walk away and she left him smoldering
now, just as she'd done then.

She'd been just a teen the summer she'd left LaGrange.
He'd been four . . . no five . . . years older, fresh from college,
certain he'd known everything he – and she – had needed to
know. What neither of them could have predicted was that
she'd leave town with rodeo trash like Tyge LaMonte and take
a piece of Cade's heart and soul with her. He hadn't been in
love with her. She was still too young and he had too much to
accomplish, his version of conquering the world he supposed,
but he'd always thought ... someday. And he had been furious
at her lack of judgement where LaMonte was concerned.

He'd tracked her progress through her years on the circuit,
of course, even when he'd been roping and living as wildly as he
could while keeping his edge in competition. Later his position

as director of a small but high-profile professional rodeo association required that he know 'who was who' in the rodeo world. That was especially true now when he was even more directly in *her* world. In spite of her early-years relationship with a loser like LaMonte, her barrel racing career in its entirety had been stellar. He'd told himself often that her success was the only reason he kept tabs on her, so often he'd almost come to believe it. Almost, but not quite.

Cade stared after her way too long, noting legs that looked damned good in the kind of heels he'd never seen on any rodeo grounds. A slim-fitting dress that hugged her slender back and waist swirled into frothy layers just below her hips. He couldn't have said what the material was called but he sure as hell could've described the way it flirted with the flesh just above the back of her knees.

With a physical reaction he wouldn't acknowledge, he turned to search the dance floor for a partner who wouldn't remind him of Malone.

Two hours later, Cade acknowledged failure. Not a single woman reminded him of Malone but every damned one of them reminded him that she was *not* Malone. Not the woman he wanted to hold in his arms as he waltzed, two-stepped and even line danced to the music. Not the woman he wanted to touch, to kiss, to hold ever tighter. And the music, itself – from song to song – was a slight but definite throb of heartbeat, heartache . . . and regret.

Some hours later, with a sincere word of congratulations to the bride and groom, Cade sought the sanctuary of the bungalow that had been assigned to him. He'd get up early, he thought as he stretched out in the dark, even earlier than he'd planned, and be out of here and on the road by first light. His Australian Shepherd padded lightly around the room finally settling quietly on the rug beside his bed. Within moments, Townsend's breathing evened into sleep. Cade's, unfortunately, did not.

DAY WAS BARELY BREAKING as Malone waited quietly in the hall of the barn while Avery's resident veterinarian glanced through her gelding's medical history, though she felt certain he'd read it thoroughly when she'd scanned and e-mailed it a week ago. The report was pages long and represented several months of treatment and frustration. When Tucker finally looked up at her, she caught and held her breath, both hopeful and fearful in the same instant.

"I'm not going to say he's wrong, Malone, but I don't entirely know that I think he's right, either. EPM is hard to diagnose and harder to treat. I will tell you the onset is rarely, if ever, as fast as what this guy experienced. You say he pulled a check for you and two days later he could hardly move?"

"We were at Waco. I hand-walked him the day after he ran and he was more than fine, dancing at the end of the lead line. When I got him out of the stall the next morning to load up and head home, he was all but dragging his left leg. I had a local vet look at him but he couldn't find anything wrong. Mylo seemed better after a day or two and I was able to get him home, to my own vet, but soon he quit eating and worsened after that."

"Just doesn't fit the EPM profile although some other things do, such as the muscle atrophy along the left hip and spasticity when walking. And nothing happened during that run?"

"It was flawless. He slipped and fell two weeks before that, but he wasn't hurt. We picked ourselves up and walked out of the arena and he showed absolutely no ill effects. We pulled checks at our next two runs, placing first in one and second in the other."

Tucker glanced down at the papers he held, then back at the animal. "Well, I'm glad you brought him to me. I won't promise I can cure whatever is happening, but I'll give it one hundred percent and you know he'll be well cared for here."

"I do." Malone fought tears and the lump in her throat. "I hate to leave him but I'm committed to a good string of big-money rodeos between here and Oklahoma City then I'll have to head right back for the southeastern circuit finals. I've got four outside horses from really good customers. I can't let them down and the trailer time would be too hard on Mylo. It would be selfish to take him with me."

Theirs was one of the few associations that allowed its members to compete in more than one circuit. Due to her own determination and a grueling schedule, she was the first to make the finals in both circuits, the southwest where she'd made her home for years and the southeast which had been home so long ago, where she'd first competed and which some-times beckoned still. Until he was well, she could not force Mylo to keep that grueling schedule with her.

"I'll take care of him, Malone," he said. "The best care possible."

Not trusting her voice, she just nodded as she ran a hand down the gelding's head before wrapping both arms around his neck.

Reluctantly, she stepped back as Tucker returned the silvery gray to his stall and latched the door.

Already feeling a sense of loss, Malone crossed to the next stall to put a halter on Jaz. She led the big sorrel mare out of the barn and into the morning, toward the truck and trailer. It was still early, still chilly, that peaceful time of day she enjoyed most when the sun was just barely over the horizon. She wanted to be gone before any of the other wedding guests roused themselves. Not even to herself would she admit there was only one person she hoped to avoid. With any luck at all, Cade Delaney was sleeping off a good time.

Malone smiled at the sight of Avery propped against the hood of her truck, two steaming mugs in her hands and a black cat twining around her dusty boots. At her approach, Avery pushed away from the truck and handed her one of the mugs.

"What in the world is the bride doing up at this hour?" Malone eyed Avery over an appreciative sip of coffee that tasted every bit as heavenly as it smelled.

Avery chuckled. "I couldn't keep my eyes from opening. I'll nap on the plane."

"I can't believe you're actually taking time for a honeymoon."

"I can't either, really. I've always wanted to see Wales but never dreamed I really would. Dirks smooth talked me into it."

"Good for Dirks. And good for you for finding a way to trust again."

Avery nodded. She would know where Malone's thoughts had gone. "It wasn't easy, but if I can, you can."

"I'd have to want to," Malone said lightly, "and I don't." To take any sting out of her response, she added with real honesty, "I'm too happy with my life now – finally – to risk changing anything."

As if on cue, the door to the guest cabin closest to them opened and Malone caught a glimpse of Cade in her peripheral vision as he stepped through with a small tote in hand. Damn. And he naturally turned toward his hostess and Malone. Double damn.

A beautiful dog, Australian Shepherd, from the coat and color, walked beside him. She automatically glanced at the black cat but Trouble showed no sign of interest, much less alarm. Of course, the cat, that belonged to another of Avery's friends was considered to be something of a hero, credited with abilities that certainly would not lend themselves to his cowering in fright at a mere dog.

"Avery. Malone." Cade greeted them both in the same pleasant tone.

Avery's eyes widened. "You two know each other . . . but, of course, I forget. You both make your living in rodeo."

Before Malone could speak, before she could casually agree as she intended, Cade said, "We knew each other before that." His gaze caught on Malone's. "Long before."

Mercifully that silver gaze moved on to Jaz standing quietly on her lead line. "Nice mare. Yours?"

Malone let a little of the tension ease from her shoulders. "Yes. I actually got her here last summer. She's been pulling some nice checks since January when I started hauling her in earnest. She's been at the top of my string the last couple of months. I'm very grateful to Avery and her team for allowing me to have her."

"We were glad to match her with you." Avery's expression remained curious at the early nuances of their exchange, but to Malone's relief she asked no questions. "We've watched your success, the videos you've posted, with a lot of pride at her accomplishments. It's clear your first assessment was right. She loves her job."

Starting to feel antsy under Cade's steady regard, Malone handed her the empty mug. "I appreciate the coffee and the wedding was absolutely lovely. I'm going to get my girl loaded and head out. I've got a full week ahead of me."

"Both Dirks and I were happy that you could be here. I put a thermos of coffee in the front of your truck but we'd love for you to have breakfast before you leave. Dirks was already poking around in the kitchen when I stepped out. He's planning to feed anyone who is awake enough to eat."

No way was Malone spending the next couple hours with Cade watching her. She declined with a smile and thanks and led Jaz around to the side of the trailer. To her consternation, Cade and his dog followed. Without asking, Cade lowered the loading ramp with quiet efficiency.

Not wanting to sound as ungrateful as she felt, she murmured thanks she didn't feel. She'd been taking care of herself for a long time.

"Where are you headed?"

Cade's question surprised her, not the words, but the fact that he'd asked. And she didn't want to tell him but he'd find out if he wanted to anyway.

"LaGrange."

His brows lifted at that. "Opposite direction of Oklahoma." She knew the comment wasn't nearly as casual as it seemed. LaGrange had once been home to both of them, but he'd know her mother had died and her father had remarried, sold their property there, and moved out of state. She certainly wasn't about to ask how he knew she was entered in Oklahoma City in little more than a week. He might be their new Director of Operations but exactly what competitor was entered where wasn't something anyone would expect him to know. In the end, she simply answered his question as if there were no unhappy history between them.

"Granddad left me his place. I suspect there are some things of his I'll want to keep so I need a day or two to sort through before I call a realtor to list it."

"I heard you'd lost him." All of the edge had left his expression and his voice. "I know that hurt."

"It did, yes." She didn't need to ask how he'd known. Her granddad's place bordered the Delaney property and Cade and his family were probably still very close. He hadn't disappointed, hadn't shamed his parents as she had hers.

For the next few minutes she focused on loading Jaz but she knew Cade was still there, still watching and wasn't the least surprised when he helped her raise the ramp and secure the doors.

She turned to face him, feeling unexpectedly awkward. "Thanks for the help. I'll see you down the road, I guess."

"Yes." That was all he said and she couldn't read a thing in his expression. Or maybe she just didn't want to. He stepped back as she climbed up into the cab of her truck, a freightliner, up to the weight of her trailer loaded with horses.

INTERESTING THING ABOUT HUMANS, *they do not always say in words what is communicated in their eyes and their expressions. While these two friends of my Ms. Gorgeous dance around their emotions, I shall stroll about the rather large truck and equally massive trailer to ensure all is in good repair and safe for the long haul. That's western speak for the lengthy trip ahead.*

I've learned through my cases to-date that the female of the human species is as capable and competent as any male, however, there is a point of chivalry in any real male that simply requires this extra vigilance on their behalf. Indeed, I noticed Mr. Silver Eyes surreptitiously eyeing the tires of her rig to ensure they are up to the trip.

All of the various side compartments, which I learned during my previous sojourn at Summer Valley Ranch contain various grains and supplements as well as buckets and fans and extension cords or other equipages, seem securely closed.

Ah, but wait. What's this? As I turn the corner to peruse the opposite side, an inch or two of faded denim along with worn leather boots disappear beneath a long, narrow access that is slowly lowered but not closed tight. Ms. Rodeo is about to have a fare-dodger and I can see very little but a pair of eyes staring back at me! Those eyes are dulled by some emotion, at best despair, at worst something more ominous. I can't tell if this is friend or foe and cannot leave Ms. Rodeo to be taken unaware somewhere down the road, perhaps at an isolated rest stop. I'd best warn Mr. Silver Eyes.

Oh, my! The truck engine has started with a bit of a roar and there is no time. I leap forward praying that the opening is wide enough for me to slip through and that the somber-eyed human does not discern my intent in time to lower the metal hatch even more.

There I'm in! And just in the nick of time, as the truck and trailer move forward. Well, this was certainly not my plan for the day. As soon as possible, I will need to let my precious Tammy Lynn, the human who claims me as her very own moggy, know my whereabouts.

For now, my excellent night vision shifts into gear and I study the human who stares back at me with no small measure of consternation.

End of excerpt from *Turning for Trouble*
by Susan Y. Tanner
Trouble Cat Mysteries #7

TROUBLE CAT MYSTERIES

Please join our Trouble Cat Mysteries page on Facebook:
fb.me/TroubleCatMysteries

www.troublecatmysteries.com

Familiar Trouble | Carolyn Haines
Trouble in Dixie | Rebecca Barrett
Trouble in Tallahassee | Claire Matturro
Trouble in Summer Valley | Susan Y. Tanner
Small Town Trouble | Laura Benedict
Trouble in Paradise | Rebecca Barrett
Turning for Trouble | Susan Y. Tanner
Trouble's Wedding Caper | Jen Talty

TROUBLE'S DOUBLE CONTEST WINNER
Leo

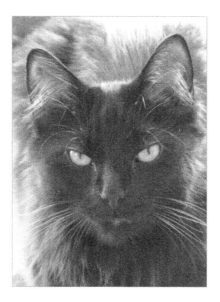

Leo began his life with his four brothers in a pile of trash from the building of my new home. While going to water my garden one morning, I found five black kittens playing on the scrap wood and things. We rescued them (and a litter that we found in my garage as well). Leo was the last one we caught. He was very cautious. And he also escaped the next day while we had them all out, feeding and loving them.

I decided to keep the only short-hair. But Leo evaded capture and while the others found homes. When the contractor came with a dumpster to get the pile and haul to the dump, I was out there, trying to find the little kitten, but there we so many nails in boards and I didn't want to hurt him. Luckily, I saw him escape after the first scoop of his old home. He lived in our neighbor's shed. She called him Houdini, because of his escaping skills.

We fed him and tried to get him to come to us, but he wouldn't. We did play with him and he was the cutest thing with the longest whiskers and tufts of fur! By the time we did catch him, I'd fallen in love and kept both of them. We gave him what we considered a royal name, because he just had such royal presence. Leo the Lion King.

Leo's eyes are very light, a bit more gold than his brother, Trouble. He has the most beautiful, singsong voice. I had no idea he would learn how to open doors! He's so funny. If I'm going into my room and I call him, he comes running and jumps on my bed; it's time for "Sucky Love". Our special time together where I give him a massage and also rub the area just above his tail and his butt goes up in the air and he sucks on my bed like it's his mama.

He's so gentle and loves us so much. He is very curious and tilts his head, trying to figure things out. He loves water dripping in the sink, but balks at his baths, although all he does is complain, but he knows he's super-handsome afterwards. I must say he is a bit of a klutz though. He loses his balance and sometimes misses his goal as he's leaping.

Ah, but Leo can fly! His fur is so long under his armpits, that when he jumps, it looks like wings! And he can soar quite a distance with those Armpit Wings! Leo has a hate/hate relationship with the mailman and delivery people. You know when someone is coming to the door because Leo GROWLS at them! I mean growls like a dog!

I was not the one that caught Leo, my neighbor Louanne did. For some reason, of all the people, he has a unique relationship with her. He keeps his distance. But what is so funny is that he will watch out the window as people behind us, around us and other things are going on, but the look on his face when he spots Louanne from a distance is hilarious! His head goes back, then forward, checking to see if it's her, then he growls!

Leo does not like me to leave on vacation. A weekend with the girls and we're up in the mountains, laughing and talking and my phone rings. I answer and my daughter announces, "Leo needs to speak to you!" So there I am on the phone, talking to Leo while my friends are rolling laughing.

I get at least one phone call a day from Leo, where we express how much we miss each other. Leo Love is precious! I can't imagine my life without my Fluff of Love! (Yeah, I've got lots of nicknames for him). Luckily, he has no desire to leave our home and venture into the scary outside world.

— TINA ANDERSON

Made in the USA
Las Vegas, NV
19 January 2023

65905208R00134